*All That
Work
and Still
No Boys*

The

Iowa

Short

Fiction

Award

In honor of James O. Freedman

University of

Iowa Press

Iowa City

Kathryn Ma

All That Work and Still No Boys

University of Iowa Press, Iowa City 52242

Copyright © 2009 by Kathryn Ma

www.uiowapress.org

Printed in the United States of America

The University of Iowa Press is a member of Green Press
Initiative and is committed to preserving natural resources.

Printed on acid-free paper

ISBN-13: 978-1-58729-822-6
ISBN-10: 1-58729-822-8
LCCN: 2009923716

For my daughters

Contents

ACKNOWLEDGMENTS

For early support and encouragement, I am grateful to the Bread Loaf Writers' Conference. I also found abundant community at the Tin House Summer Writers Workshop.

To the many teachers, fellow writers, family members, and friends who have supported me in this work, I offer thanks for your generosity and friendship.

I am indebted as a reader and a writer to Holly Carver and her colleagues at the University of Iowa Press and to the Iowa Writers' Workshop.

Thank you to the editors of the publications in which my stories have appeared, including the following: "What I Know Now" in the *Antioch Review*; "Prank" in the *Kenyon Review*; "Mrs. Zhao and Mrs. Wu" in the *Portland Review*; "For Sale By Owner" in *Prairie Schooner*; "All That Work and Still No Boys" (winner of the 2008 David Nathan Meyerson Prize for Fiction) and "Dougie" in *Southwest Review*; "Gratitude" in the *Threepenny Review*; and "The Long Way Home" in *TriQuarterly*. Your dedication and commitment kept my spirit alive.

To my husband, Sanford Kingsley, I give daily thanks for your faith and love.

All That
Work
and Still
No Boys

Barbara's mother needs a new kidney, and Lawrence is the best match.

"No, no," says her mother. "One of the girls will be fine."

"It's okay, Ma," says Lawrence. Barbara sees him reach for something small at the top of Ma's shelf, so she knows it's costing him to sound enthusiastic. It's an old family habit, lying while turning away. "I've got two, way more than I need. You take one. I want you to have it."

Ma nods but doesn't answer, another deft deception, the yes that's really a no. Ma has no intention of letting him give her a kidney. She's already made that perfectly clear to Barbara. She's got four daughters but only one Lawrence. She wants the girls to draw straws from the second-best broom in the house.

"Let's have lunch," says Ma. "I've got everything ready." Lawrence sets the table while Barbara serves the soup. The battle's under way, and Barbara needs to keep her strength up.

She takes her mother to see the doctor once again.

"Mrs. Yin," says Dr. Hu kindly, "it's really not a matter of patient discretion. The tests tell us that Lawrence is the best family match. He's young and healthy and should have no problem relying on his remaining kidney for the rest of his life."

Up on the examining table, Ma swings her legs like a girl on the playground kicking higher. The paper underneath her makes a cheerful crunch. Barbara sits in the corner under the color illustrations of kidneys, heart, and stomach, which she's glad she doesn't have to look at, not facing them like her mother, though Ma is smiling brightly at handsome Dr. Hu. For such an ill woman, she looks surprisingly healthy—stout and pink, with thick, short hair dyed inky black. "I've been feeling a lot better," she tells him. "Maybe an operation isn't necessary at all."

This is not new, what she is claiming. Dr. Hu has heard it from her before. He looks at Barbara, coconspirator in their plan to save Ma's life. Make her do it, his eyes are flashing. Barbara bends her head to hide her embarrassment and frustration. Dr. Hu has no right to expect a miracle from Barbara. After all, he's Chinese too: he knows what it's like to stare up at a mountain.

"Any luck?" asks Tracy when she calls. She is sixteen months younger than Barbara and does her best to share the load. In nine years, their mother had five children: Barbara, Tracy, Janet, Robin, and Lawrence, and Barbara, as the oldest, helped Ma take care of them all. Tracy groans when Barbara reports that Ma hasn't changed her mind. "Did you have the doctor tell her again about how the best match means the least chance of rejection?"

"I asked him again, and he told her again."

"And did you have him remind her that Lawrence is the same blood type?"

"You take her next time. Since you know all the right questions."

Tracy apologizes. They're both exhausted. They take turns driving to see Ma every other weekend. It's too far to drive and too short to fly so of course they drive, three hours in traffic each way. Barbara and Tracy are in San Francisco. Ma's in the foothills east of Sacramento. The others live far away, except for Lawrence; he lives five miles from Ma.

"Dr. Hu said that if the donor isn't a good match, her own defense system might act to reject a 'foreign invader.' And Ma sort of sniffed at him and said, 'We Chinese. We let everybody in.'"

Tracy laughs. She's probably sitting up on her roof. She's got a little deck up there with two metal chairs and a tiny round table; Barbara thinks she imagines herself in Paris. Tracy looks like a Parisian, small-boned and upright. She lives with her partner, Heather, in the roomy upstairs flat, and they rent the lower unit to four women just out of college. I'd feel lonely without more girls around, says Tracy. Barbara's own house is the realm of men: her husband, Thomas, and their two teenage sons. When Josh was born, Ma sent Barbara a bouquet of red refrigerator roses, probably the only time Ma ever did such an extravagant thing. Janet didn't get flowers when the very first grandchild, her daughter Celia, was born. After Josh arrived, "Pressure's off of us now," the rest of the sisters cracked.

"Ma's all there," says Tracy. "Every last synapse is firing."

"Straight at us."

"I read something the other day. It takes three daughters to stay out of a nursing home. If you've got fewer than three daughters, odds are you'll die in an institution."

"I'm screwed then," says Barbara. Josh and Noah, she knows they love her, but will they take care of her the way a daughter would? She tries to imagine her boys as grown men, and the thought panics her briefly. She is grateful that they will leave her only a day at a time; a sudden parting would be something awful, but a slow untethering every mother must expect. Her father died without the merest warning, and the shock of his departure still makes Barbara catch her breath.

"That's why I married another woman," says Tracy. "Men die on you but women don't. I may not have daughters but I won't be stranded."

"Like Ma," says Barbara.

"Like Ma." They rest a moment, thinking of their father. One year gone, and the space he occupied grows ever larger. When she thinks of her father—not of his death but of his amused way of speaking, with a measured cadence and a tenor's pitch, and of his old flannel shirts and worn corduroy trousers, and of the way he smelled, like cotton and paper—Barbara feels a soft and pleasant ache, like the soreness in her calves after a long hike in the hills. Sometimes, if she's alone, she pulls out a second chair at the kitchen table and pours a second cup of tea that seems to stay warm longer than her own does. It brightens Barbara, the presence of the missing. She accepts that he's gone though. She hasn't started talking to that empty chair yet.

"How would Dad handle the situation?"

"He'd be smart enough to know that he couldn't *tell* her."

"She has to decide for herself," agrees Barbara.

"He might not talk about it. Give her time, let her come to her own conclusion."

"Dad was always patient," says Barbara. Ma's time is running out.

On Saturday, Barbara drives to Lawrence's before going to see Ma. He and Jenny are building a brand-new house in the long spill of foothills between the valley and the Sierra. The project's just getting started; they're drilling the water well. For now, they're renting a manicured ranch house in a neighborhood full of cul-de-sacs where Barbara often turns wrong at night. It's a hundred and two by the time Barbara gets there, so she and Lawrence change into bathing suits and sit on the steps of the backyard pool to talk. Barbara glories in the heat and the lapping water; she's forgotten how wonderfully the sun can roast one dry. The baseball cap Lawrence lent her she got wet when she plopped into the water, and now she feels it shrunken and snug around her head. All summer in foggy San Francisco, Barbara has walked circles in her kitchen, mostly on the phone with one sister or another or making meals for her family that she pre-eats at five o'clock. She's grown a soft ring of fat around her middle; she feels it bulging inside her frayed black suit like a life preserver threatening to tip her over, so buoyant she's become from feeding her worries like children. As Ma has dwindled, Barbara has fattened. She wonders if her body knows something she doesn't, like famine is coming or the Big One is going to hit.

"Come with me to Ma's," says Barbara. "We can talk to her together."

"It's no good. She'd rather get one from a stranger."

"It won't be a good match."

"Strangers can be just as good as family."

Barbara studies the water, feeling the edges of his words in her mind the way a careful woman tests the carving knife. In the silence Lawrence sneezes, which she takes as a sign that he doesn't mean what he said.

"She might sit on the list five years or longer."

"And anyway," says Lawrence, "I'm the youngest so Ma doesn't listen to me."

"You're the son."

"With five fucking mothers." Lawrence windmills his arms to rile up the water. A raft at the other end of the pool sets to rocking. "I told her I'd do it. If she wants it, she can have it. What more do you want me to say?"

"It's really awkward," says Barbara, "but I think you need to just keep making the offer." The sisters had discussed it and decided that Barbara should put this proposal to Lawrence. He's not selling the idea, said Janet, who's in branding. He needs to make the case and not take no for an answer.

"I can't. It was hard enough to tell her the first time. I wrote her a letter too, did you know that?"

Barbara shakes her head.

"Ma didn't tell you? Because if one of you knows, then all four have heard it. 'What about Lawrence?'" He mimics the four of them uncomfortably well. "'Did he really tell Ma she could have one of his, or did he duck his head and mumble when he said it?'"

"I know you offered, but—"

"I told her twice. It's Ma's decision now."

Barbara slides one step lower until the water comes up to her chin. She doesn't want to enrage Lawrence, but they don't have time to think of each other's feelings. "You know how when we used to go to a restaurant with Uncle Bill, he and Dad would always argue over the check? Even when it was Uncle Bill's turn to pay, Dad would make a big show of reaching for the check and insisting he wanted to host?"

Lawrence looks down at her from the step above. She can't see his eyes behind his sunglasses, which gives her the courage to not look away. "Are you comparing my kidney to the dinner bill?" he says. "To the $24.95 for the Peking duck special?"

"It's a Chinese thing," says Barbara. "They used to argue back and forth for a good ten minutes until Dad let Uncle Bill lay his Visa card down on the tray." Which wasn't very often. Their father liked paying for everyone else, even when money was tight and the girls were passing down holey sneakers.

"It's a pride thing," says Barbara.

"She's not too proud to take one of yours," says Lawrence. He pokes his finger into her back, at her kidney. Barbara grabs his finger and holds it. "I don't see any of you stepping up to the plate."

"Tracy thinks it's funny that you're the best match."

"Since I almost wasn't born," Lawrence completes her thought. The family story by now is mythic, and Barbara's so sick of it that she swings his hand by his finger to distract him. "Cut it out," says Lawrence, but Barbara keeps swinging until he pulls his hand out, dripping, and flicks the water in her face. "Ma's gone mad," he says, "and you know why? You guys drove her crazy just like you do to me."

Barbara nods thoughtfully. He's right to complain; she knows it. They can't help themselves; they have clucked over their little brother for thirty-six years with no prospect of stopping. Once, when he was four, on a nice warm summer day, Barbara put him on the back of her bike and told him to stick his feet out, straight out like a Christmas tree or a robot, and then pedaled down the block to take him to the swim club. In front of the neighbors' house, their nasty Dalmatian came dashing out, and Lawrence, screaming, stuck his big bare foot right into the back wheel spokes. Ma went quiet when she was summoned by the neighbor; that's how Barbara knew how much damage she had done. After that, she was always careful. She reaches under the water and grabs his left ankle, feels for the scar from her bicycle spokes and finds it. Lawrence puts his hands on her shoulders, and she knows what's coming next, but anyway, she lets him. Swiftly he dunks her, and she comes up sputtering, reaching over her head to snatch his cap away. They twist into the water and race down the length of the pool, Lawrence letting her win with a faked cramp right before the finish. Then they float, talking of other things, the house Lawrence and Jenny are building and the dog they plan to get as soon as it's finished. Jenny comes home with sandwiches and beer, and they eat, hanging off the edge of the pool, using the curb as their tabletop and the deep end as their napkin. Jenny tells Barbara about a problem she's having at work, and Barbara does her best not to sound like a fuddy-duddy. Nobody brings up the subject of Ma again.

After lunch, Jenny changes back into her pink and yellow sundress and goes to meet a friend while Lawrence and Barbara drive out to look at the land, a welcome excuse, thinks Barbara, to put off dealing with Ma. They walk the dry brown scape, kicking up dust and counting out their paces. He shows her two test holes put down by the water well contractor. There should be plenty of groundwater, but they haven't found the right place to drill for their well just yet. The drilling contractor shows up and spends a long time talking to Lawrence about the other wells in the area. "We'll find you a nice fat aquifer," he promises Lawrence, and Barbara hears the frustration in his voice. She worries that Lawrence has made a bad investment; without enough water, what will his land be worth? Next to the drilling rig a hole in the ground beckons; she wants to lie on her stomach and look straight down into the earth. Maybe she will discover something that everyone else has missed, but when she moves toward it, the contractor waves her off. "It's small but deep," he warns. She backs away and waits for Lawrence to drive her to her car. It's so late by the time Barbara gets to Ma's house that she has to stay for dinner, dragging up cheerful things to say to Ma about the boys and her part-time work as a city planner. She drives home in the dark, arriving after midnight. She has accomplished nothing helpful today.

———

Ma reheats a piece of toast and sits alone in her kitchen. She thinks it's obvious that one of the girls should be the donor. Barbara, for instance. She's suspicious of the tests that claim Lawrence is the best match, for after all, in the well-ordered family, the girls take after their mother. Barbara's life has proven that to be true. Like Ma, she is hard-working and devoted to her children, and she knows that women have to be tougher than men. When Edwin died so suddenly at the office, Barbara, like Ma, was the only one who didn't fall apart. Lawrence was the worst, crying his eyes out over the polished coffin. He was weeping so hard he couldn't take his turn at the lectern, so Edwin was sent off with only girls to praise him. Still, Ma has to admit, the girls did a good job re-telling the life of their father. Janet is very good at those sorts of things. She knows how to tell a long story quickly. And Tracy was good too. She's a radio personality (how Ma loves that phrase!). She grabs all kinds of words and puts them together in short, staccato sentences that don't last very long in their meaning but do the trick in the moment. Ma likes that sort of American way of speaking, fast bursts that don't linger around to bother her like flies buzzing against a shut window. Ma's head is a kind of echo chamber where remarks people have made to her live on for years of pricking judgment. Little things that the speaker didn't give a second thought to but that Ma can't forget, caught as they are in the chamber. Ma's sixth grade teacher saying, "You're good at math so your brother must be even better." Her first boyfriend's sister who snuck up on them kissing and called Ma a catfish for puckering up like she did. And Edwin's mother: "Your breasts are too small. If you get on top you can make them look bigger." Ma can't help herself: she often returns to her echo chamber to hear those old comments and remember how she overcame them. She is proud that she took each insult as a chance to improve. Barbara's like that too. She doesn't let criticism stop her from trying. With such a practical approach to life, Ma is certain that if Barbara were to be her donor, things would work out without incident or worry. Capable people make their own solutions. Ma and Barbara have been good at that for years.

Ma wonders briefly if the girls think she's giving up. As in, what's the point in going through with the operation? Edwin is gone and the children all grown. But that's not the case: Ma wants to live longer. Not so badly that Lawrence should have to suffer. Even a little risk isn't worth taking. With Edwin gone, there's only Lawrence.

Barbara calls a family meeting, minus Ma so they can sort out their crisis. Robin flies in from Atlanta, and Janet arrives from Boston. Lawrence calls to say he can't come till tomorrow; a back-hoe on his property accidentally crashed into a pickup.

"Lo," says Tracy on the phone, which she's carried into the dining room. She calls him Lo, his childhood nickname. They are all sitting around the table at Tracy's, waiting for Lawrence to show up for dinner. "You were driving that backhoe, weren't you?" She smiles at her sisters and makes a face, *that's our Lawrence.* "How many times have I told you not to drive without shoes on?" Barbara flexes her ankle, remembering the bicycle spokes. "He's still playing with toys," says Tracy when she hangs up.

"Is there anything to drink in this house?" Robin asks.

"What do you call that?" says Tracy, pointing to the bottle of wine on the table.

Robin drapes an arm across the back of her chair. "Ma and Dad threw a better party than you do."

Tracy stands abruptly and goes to the hallway to rummage. "Is this what you want?" She plunks on the table a bottle of Jim Beam Black. There's an old card attached from Dad's boss one before last.

"You stole this from Dad," Robin says.

"I found it," Tracy exclaims. "In an old suitcase at the back of Dad's closet."

"He probably hid it and forgot it," says Janet.

"Or kept it for an emergency," Barbara jokes. There are only two kinds of emergencies, Dad used to tease, acts of God and Ma-made disasters. Robin grabs the bottle and goes into the kitchen for ice and two glasses, then pours a shot for herself and Janet. Barbara watches them clink glasses before anyone else has a drink. They feel left out, being so far from Ma and unable to visit as often. Their guilt has taken the form of resentment, Robin complaining as soon as she arrived that Barbara wasn't letting anyone else try to talk sense into Ma. Be my guest, Barbara had retorted, and Robin said she'd give one of hers if it ended Ma's medieval way of thinking that insulted women and made her glad she lived in Atlanta. She looks tired, notices Barbara. Tiny dark crescents hang softly below her eyes, and she's gotten so thin that the skirt of her suit has swiveled a quarter turn so the kick pleat hangs awkwardly down one thigh. Janet looks better, taut with exercise and sporting a glossy bob that parts for gold earrings clipped like wing nuts to her lobes.

They drink one round and drink another. Tracy gets up to sauté some chicken. She's no good at the stove; her partner, Heather, does all the cooking. Barbara would get to her feet and help, but the liquor has taken hold, and she's enjoying the rare release. She and her sisters are exquisitely attuned to one another's signals—who's miffed, who's feeling righteous, whose turn it is to placate—and Barbara usually scans for trouble, but tonight she lets Robin pour her another shot. When the meal arrives, bread and salad and chicken, the four eat mostly with their fingers, picking croutons out of the bowl and pieces of avocado.

"I can't believe she would let one of us be a donor but not Lawrence," one of them says for the thousandth time. Barbara, her head resting for an instant against the back of her chair, isn't sure whether it's Janet or Robin. "Is it Dad, do you think? Is that why she's gone crazy?"

"Ma was always like this," says Tracy. "Are you forgetting why she had Lo in the first place?"

Robin groans, or maybe it's Janet. Barbara stands and heads up to the rooftop; Robin and Janet follow with the bottle in Janet's hand.

"Be careful," Tracy yells as they open the door and step out onto the roof. There's no wall and no railing either. Tracy lives in a better neighborhood than Barbara; the fog hasn't followed Barbara here tonight. There's nothing to look at but other rooftops, though there's a warm breeze blowing and they can hear music coming from a party below. On the little Parisian table an ashtray and cigarettes appear, and the sisters sit down to smoke, Robin and Janet sharing a third chair that Tracy has dragged up the stairs. Robin keeps laughing as she tries to stay on the seat.

"It's three A.M. in Boston," says Janet.

"And your ass is just as wide here as it is there." Robin hitches half her butt back onto the chair.

"Sit here," offers Barbara, rising.

"Stop it," says Robin. "Just stop *doing* for the rest of us all the time."

"Leave her alone," Tracy cuts in.

"It's exhausting. It's annoying. Ask Lawrence. He'll tell you. She's been driving up there to mope around his house, begging him to prostrate himself before Ma. I agree with Lawrence. It's Ma's decision and we can't do anything about it until she realizes she's going to die unless she gets a new one. Making the rest of us feel bad isn't going to bring Ma to that conclusion any faster."

Barbara can't say anything, but it doesn't matter because Tracy has stuck her arm across the table and knocked Robin's glass off the table. The glass rolls on the tar-and-gravel rooftop toward the edge of Tracy's house, hangs for a second, then drops. They all four turn to hear it shatter, but just at the moment it should be hitting the sidewalk, somebody opens the door to the neighbor's party, and music and voices briefly take over.

"I'll go," says Janet, like a command, and she disappears down the stairs. The others wait, not looking at each other or uttering a word. When trouble brews, they always fall silent. Tempers might flare for a brief exchange of opinion, but muteness is the haven for which they all scurry when a truth pops out and can't be popped back in. Only Dad tried to break them of the habit, singing and joking if one of the girls went sullen. It's not good for digestion to swallow your words, he would tell them, and poke them in the belly until they yelled at him to cut it out. You have a voice! Dad would shout, raising an open hand in triumph. The only one he left alone was Lawrence, but Lawrence was the boy and the opposite of his sisters. Most of the time he was quiet until he got mad: then he cursed and shoved them away.

"Look!" says Janet when she returns to the rooftop. She holds up the unbroken glass. They are above the streetlamps but still the glass is glinting, from what source, Barbara cannot tell; there's neither lamplight nor moonlight casting down on their heads. She tries to stand up to clear the fog descending.

"I thought you lived on the sunny side of town," she says.

"She can't drive home." Somebody else is talking.

"And I brought this," says Janet. There is mirth in her voice and trouble. She holds up four broom straws, like cards just dealt to her hand. "Who wants to draw first?"

"That's not funny," says Tracy sharply. "It's not a crapshoot. It's not Russian roulette. Doctors decide these things. If it's Lawrence, it's Lawrence."

"Just for fun," cajoles Janet. "We won't tell Ma we did it."

"Me first," says Barbara, wanting after all to be a good sport for her sisters. She draws, and then Janet holds out the handful to Tracy, who scowls and shakes her head no. Robin reaches a lazy arm forward. She draws the short one. Nobody says a word.

"Ha," Robin finally utters, but before she throws it down, she swallows. The light that a moment ago lit the whiskey glass, that miraculous glass with its bounce and its story, has gone away, and now they sit in darkness.

"It's not for real," says Barbara to reassure her.

"Shut up," says Robin and jerks the table toward her. Barbara's glass falls to the roof and breaks. When the end of the weekend comes, nothing has been decided.

Ma lies on the table hooked up to her kindred machines. Like family they are, salvation and burden. A caregiver brings her three times a week. Ma uses the services of whomever the agency sends. The woman at the agency was surprised at Ma's request that she not keep sending the same person week after week. Most of our clients want to bond with their helpers, she said to Ma. Are you sure you don't want me to find one lady to help you? I have enough daughters! Ma came close to shouting. What a relief she feels when they send another stranger because then she can relax, knowing that as long as a stranger and not a daughter is watching, the indignity of her circumstance won't linger beyond the day.

Ma tells her daughters that she doesn't mind her regular treatments. It's just a little plumbing, is how she describes it. Flushing my toilet, she sometimes jokes to her friends, who hide their teeth behind their hands at such remarks and giggle like schoolgirls sharing what little they know or have guessed about sex. Ma doesn't use such pungent language with her daughters. They might remember her by those words alone and forget to recall her better nature.

Lately, lying on the table, letting the waste wash away, Ma feels afraid. She used to enter willingly the echo chamber in her brain. It didn't scare her to hear the old judgments because she knew she had done her best to overcome them. But these days the words boom a little louder, with truth-telling sharper and deeper than Ma recalled. She would like to close the chamber if she could, but instead, every time she lies down on the table, the door to the echo chamber swings wide open. All she can think of is how her life might have been different, what she could have done better, what she wished she could take back. The biggest shame she nurses is how she failed her husband. Many times she complained to Edwin about money. She pushed him to go to his boss to ask for more work, which would mean a bigger raise. He was a researcher; she thought he should run the department. She didn't do enough for Edwin's mother. She should have praised his talents more often to all of her friends. She kept house for him but should have been better tempered. When they wanted a son, she gave him only daughters. And then, by the time Edwin was delighted with the four girls and insisted to his wife that he was happy with girls and didn't want any more children, she tricked him into trying again and had a son who now refuses to have any children. Edwin, thinks Ma, her eyes closed and burning.

Edwin wasn't angry with her when he learned she was pregnant again. He had asked her to stop trying. She had miscarried twice after Robin was born. Daughters are a blessing, he had tried to convince her. They will take care of us in our old age. Ma's doctor told her she had to stop. But then her mother's sister came to visit. She was only a half sister, and Ma didn't like her, but it was expected that she and Edwin would host. Auntie came in and sat herself on their sofa. Looked at the four girls lined up to greet her. Shook her head and clucked like a chicken. "All that work," she said to Ma with pity. "All that work and still no boys."

Every minute after that during Auntie's visit, with every chore Ma performed, the chamber echoed. She yearned for her own mother to come screeching back to life, to fly through the open window, pull the half sister's nose, and push her out into the street. Her girls were good girls, more than enough for Edwin. But her mother did not come flying back through the window. Instead, her voice came into the chamber and joined the other echoes. "This is my son," Ma remembered her mother boasting when the neighbors brought red eggs to welcome Ma's little brother. It was true, what Auntie succinctly said. No matter what anyone said about girls, how daughters were just as good as sons or even better, they didn't believe it, not fully, deep down. They were speaking lies when they praised her daughters, and their lies burned Ma like swallowed acid. When Lawrence was finally born and the doctor handed him to his father, Ma watched with pride and savage anger how Edwin smiled joyfully and stroked Lawrence's little head.

"Barbara is not a match," Dr. Yin says firmly. He will not let Barbara stand in as donor. The sick feeling in Barbara's stomach subsides a little in the ripple of guilt and relief that washes through her.

"I'm sorry, Ma," Barbara says. "Please don't tell the others I went for the testing again." She fears their disdain if they find out she has offered. Ma sighs, and it sounds like a sigh of eternal disappointment. Barbara will not be the one to save her. They drive home, and Barbara is glad for the wind whipping between the open car windows. Whatever they have to say to one another will be snatched from their mouths as they try to say it. She glances at Ma, who is hunched in her seat with her eyes cast down, like she's praying. Maybe she should take Ma to her church, where they could pray together, but Barbara doesn't believe in prayer, and neither does Ma, whose beliefs are both more practical and more ancient. Unwillingly, Barbara thinks of how Ma got Lawrence, the old story that Barbara hates to hear. Ma could not have more children, the doctor had insisted. She had to stop trying or she would endanger her health. But Ma, not the doctor, knew how to take care of the problem. She found a lady who knew a woman who had the know-how to tell Ma what to do. Ma paid the woman fifty dollars, and this knowledgeable woman told Ma exactly which teas to brew, which herbs to swallow, which dates to do it on, which furniture to rearrange. She wrote certain characters on a scroll that Ma hung in the bedroom because the number of brush strokes would bring the luckiest outcome. All this Ma described to Barbara, Tracy, Janet, and Robin when they were young girls and again when they were older, even telling them about the two babies conceived after Robin who had fitfully bled away, so that the scale of the miracle—a son delivered after so many years of waiting—would be known by each of them and appreciated fully. That is why Barbara hates the story: it is not a family myth but a mother's lesson. Truth be told—and she told no one, not her husband, not Ma, not her sister Tracy—when Barbara was ready to try for children of her own, she thought about Ma's story, wondered about that woman. Asked herself if maybe she should find a practitioner of her own who could tell her what herbs to consume and which months were more auspicious to the mother who wished for a son. She didn't, of course. She's a modern woman. But the thought was there, and the base desire, moving inside her like a fetus.

When they get to Ma's house, Barbara helps her mother to bed, then goes to the kitchen to make herself a sandwich. She puts on the kettle and makes two cups of tea, then sits by herself at the table. "Daddy," she says once into the cool of the kitchen. A sharp pain in her breast has replaced the pleasant ache that she usually feels when she thinks about her father. How did he put up with Ma's stubbornness over the years? But there isn't much point in parsing her parents' marriage. No one else can know it; she knows this for certain, since she's been married herself for twenty years. Instead, she thinks of how she used to wait for her father. "I'm sorry, Ma," Barbara had cried the afternoon that she had balanced Lawrence, too young, on her bike. Ma had said nothing except to refuse Barbara's imploring to allow her to hold a wailing Lawrence while Ma drove him to the doctor's. Barbara had waited, alone and frightened, for the whole afternoon in the empty house, the younger girls having been sent to the better care of the neighbor. When her father had come home, Barbara had run to him, but Ma interrupted and called him to their bedroom. Out in the hallway on the exiled side of the door, Barbara could hear her mother's voice rising and crashing. He didn't come out, Barbara remembers. He didn't come out to comfort Barbara but let Ma punish her with cold condescension. The air conditioner switches on, and its sudden exhalation feels like a chilly slap. She stands abruptly and dumps out the second cup of tea. That pain in her breast is not grief, it is anger. Her father has left her to manage Ma by herself.

"How is your mother?" a woman has called to ask Barbara, Mrs. Li from the church where Ma is a steady member. Barbara answers briefly, having learned from Ma not to discuss personal matters.

"I'm so glad that the doctors have found a good donor."

"What?" says Barbara. "Did my mother tell you that?"

"She showed me the letter your brother Lawrence wrote. What a son!" says Mrs. Li. "Your mother is very lucky."

Barbara hangs up quickly and fumbles to call her mother. For a second, she can't even remember the number and has to glance at the list she keeps tacked to the wall. "Are you going to let Lawrence be the donor?" she demands when Ma answers.

Ma sighs. "Let's not talk about this again."

"But you told Mrs. Li that you were going to have the operation."

"Did I?" says Ma. "Mrs. Li isn't a very good friend of mine. She doesn't know the situation."

"You showed her Lawrence's letter!"

"Maybe," Ma concedes. "She brought over some cookies. I was making conversation."

"You are wearing me out!" shouts Barbara. "You won't accept help from the one person who can help you. I don't know how I can keep coming up there. You won't listen to the doctors, you won't listen to any of us. You are driving me crazy. Everybody expects me to fix this, but I can't if you won't let me. We can't keep treating Lawrence like he doesn't know what he's doing. He's married, he has a life, he has a big piece of land that he's going to build a house on. Why don't you let him help you?" It's quiet on the other end, and Barbara thinks she might have to slam down the phone and then she hears Ma crying and she has to reach for a chair. "Ma," says Barbara, her own tears rising. "I'm sorry I yelled at you. Please don't hang up."

"I might think about it," says Ma, her voice sounding wet and broken. "If you think Lawrence will be okay."

"He will, he will. The doctors all say so." Barbara hears herself promising what she can't be sure is true. She's crying harder now but Ma isn't. She has pulled herself together and is waiting for Barbara to do the same.

"We'll talk about it this weekend," says Barbara, dropping her words into a bowl of silence, and while she's at it, she pours all of her guilt into the bowl too, so that when she hangs up the phone, Barbara feels strangely airy and she leaves her kitchen to go for a walk and not think about Ma for an hour.

Ma sits alone in her bedroom. She is embarrassed that she lost control with Barbara, especially since she admitted aloud that she is starting to think she had better take Lawrence up on his offer. Barbara should not have made her say it. There was no need to browbeat the words from her mother; after all, if Barbara doesn't know what Ma is thinking, what person ever has? Most of the time she thought Edwin knew her, but a man doesn't know what it's like to live with echoes. Now Barbara's angry words have been added to the clamor. Ma will have to hear them when she lies down on the table. Edwin never yelled at her like that. Among all those voices, she has never heard Edwin's. She knows she is lucky that her husband's voice never found its way into the chamber. It's just now she realizes that all the voices trapped there are the voices of other women. Women, not men, are the ones who plague her, so why after all should she listen?

Barbara takes a day off work and drives up midweek, knowing that now is the time to get Ma to promise. Ma has told her again that she's considering the operation, but when Barbara gets close to Ma's house, she keeps on driving, thinking not of Ma but of her father. Her anger at his leaving her has not subsided; she would rather be mad at him than lose him altogether. She knows she is confused, swerving as she is between old, small betrayals and present-day burdens, but she cannot clear up her own confusion. I'm exhausted, she thinks, from driving and cajoling and running between her siblings, and she wishes she could stop but she doesn't know how to. Will you stop *doing* for us all the time? Robin had demanded, but Barbara can't; it's not in her nature. She's glad that Ma is going to agree to the operation, but it will be hard to break the news to Lawrence. Without quite realizing what she is doing, she drives without stopping until she turns down the road to Lawrence's property. There he is, sitting on the drilling rig where the land slopes upward. She walks toward him, but he doesn't return her wave. Dust settles into the sweat on her arms and legs. It's the sun, not the dust, that bears right down on the body. She holds a hand to her brow and looks over his empty land. Four capped test holes are all the work that's been done. "It's like a bad spirit is living on my land," Lawrence says when she reaches him. "It's not making any sense. The hydrogeologist can't explain it."

"There's no water at all?"

"The yields are too low. The rock tells them there should be plenty of water, but something's gone wrong. It's not pumping like it should."

"What are you going to do?"

Lawrence gets off the rig. The heat lengthens the distance between them. Every movement, every step, seems to make the air hotter. Her cheap sunglasses don't block the glare very well. "Jenny's hired a dowser," he says.

"I don't know what that is."

"A dowser. A water witcher. Who brings a divining rod and finds you your water."

"Is she a woman?" Barbara asks, though she can't think why it matters.

"No. A man. He's coming to try tomorrow."

Then why call him a witch, she wants to ask, but instead she leaves him to do her duty. When she gets to Ma's, she asks, "Are you ready?" and Ma nods yes. That's all they need to do. Barbara will spend the night and speak to Lawrence in the morning. When she closes her eyes, she feels her breath deepen. She is happy that Ma is going to live longer.

But how to tell Lawrence that Ma wants his kidney? They have coffee and rolls and drive out to the land. Jenny is with them and the moment doesn't seem right. The dowser arrives not with willow wands or a forked stick but two brass rods bent into handles. When Barbara asks, he says it's okay to walk behind, and Jenny and Barbara follow at a respectful distance as the dowser passes slowly over the dry humped ground. Barbara hears a desultory birdcall and insects clicking, but no breeze lifts her hair. Jenny's brown ponytail springs from the back of her baseball cap like a fountain. It's a sign, thinks Barbara, an omen of water. Sweat darkens the back of the dowser's blue work shirt. He is an old man, with one leg shorter than the other or maybe a weak ankle, for he drags one foot slightly to the left and behind him. As Barbara follows him, she thinks of her father sleeping. Perhaps the ancients had it wrong, and the River Styx was not a border to be crossed but a free-flowing aquifer, lifting coffins from their beds and slipping them downstream to mighty underground waterways, or maybe not the coffins but only the weightless souls that seek to journey the way a river seeks the sea, day by day, traveling into the distance, not a sudden parting but a gradual going away. The dowser stops and places a marker. She is puzzled by this; she had expected a visitation, the rods jerking downward or quivering in his hands. She thought he would yell and raise his arms in triumph or that a flock of birds would rise in a glorious swirling, but nothing like this happens. There is no sign that any change has taken place. He merely pauses in his step and leans over to thrust a metal spike into one place in the ground and then pulls out a can of spray paint and draws a circle around the spot. It's not very far from one of the test holes. Lawrence runs over looking happy and boyish. He hugs Jenny; she lifts her face to his, and, grasping arms, they dance in place for a bit. Barbara lifts her wrist to wipe a trickle of sweat from her forehead. "Ma's ready to have the operation," she says.

Jenny covers her mouth, but Lawrence doesn't flinch. He gives his sister a tiny smile. Barbara thinks of the swimming pool and the raft at the deep end, rocking. If she could, she would put her brother back on her bike and ride him like the wind to the safety of the water.

"It's okay," Lawrence tells Jenny. "We've found where our well goes." He puts his arms around his wife and turns his back to Barbara as she turns to leave their father with his last farewell on earth.

Second Child

A child is missing, the only boy in the group, one white boy out of twenty-three children. Everyone else got back to the buses on time except for Sam, twelve years old and finger-bone skinny, as soft-faced as his sister and all the rest of the girls. He'll be hard to spot among the milling tourists. His parents let him leave the gift shop while they were buying their panda T-shirts, panda hats and backpacks, counting out their money, trying to convert to dollars in their heads, and when they walked outside, he was gone. She offers cold water to the families on both buses and then walks back to the turnstile, speaks briefly to the guard, and stands by the gate to wait. The parents are scouring the park for him. If he shows up by himself, she will make sure he's all right and send him to Bus A, where she sees his sister looking nervously through the window. She feels a pinch of worry, not for Sam's safety but in case he's scared or anxious, being lost in a foreign place and not knowing the language. It would panic her to be without the words to find her way home. But Sam isn't truly lost, only a little misplaced, and the guards, when they find him, will bring him to the gate. She won't frown at him the way she did the other day with two of the girls who wandered off and made the group late for lunch. Sam didn't mean to cause trouble; he's been eager to please her. He didn't say a word for the first four days of the tour and then, in Xian, he started asking questions, speaking to her privately when the rest of the group walked away. She said it was okay, he could sit up front beside her, and gave him the window seat so he could look out at all the traffic. After that, he found her wherever they went.

She glances at her watch. They are thirty minutes behind schedule, but there's plenty of time before the farewell dinner. Tomorrow she'll go home. She'll fly home for a little rest. Her father's birthday is at the end of the week; she'll be home in time to bring him the carton of cigarettes she bought at the airport. The last day is always the longest. There's a lot to organize and nerves to settle. She'll send the families on and go alone to her gate. She checks her watch again and grimaces to the guard: these Americans, they have ideas of their own. On every tour, there are one or two who don't like to stay with the group or who criticize the schedule or ask for special treatment. It isn't the children who ask. Not the girls. But this time, there's a boy, and even though she was starting to like him, now he has made them all wait.

She walks to a bench and opens her umbrella to the sun. Her eyes empty out as she studies the paving stones. Go back and quit, that's what she ought to do. The day she gets back, she should send an e-mail to Wisconsin and make up some excuse. With her English-speaking skills, she could easily find other work in the Beijing office of a big American corporation or as assistant to the boss in a Chinese company trying to attract foreign investment. The work would be easier, and if she didn't feel like it, she wouldn't have to smile, but it would be hard to give up the money. She glances down the path and thinks about the tips. Tomorrow the families will slip her fat envelopes full of cash, the long white ones that fold and crackle and sometimes a red one from a family proud that they researched local custom. Fifty dollars American, sometimes sixty, an envelope from every family grateful for her intercession, for her very good English and that she told them to call her "Daisy." The narrow bills are sickly green and soft and thick, like cloth between her fingers. When they say good-bye, the families take her picture with their Chinese daughters, also sickly, some of them anyway, mostly unsmiling, ill with the prospect of the last stage of their tour, their "reunion visit" to their orphanage. What will it be like, she can almost hear them pleading, their eyes finding hers in mute apprehension, as if she can protect them from what is to come. Is it frightening in that place? Will I be left there? Will my real parents show up and—? But that last thought is too huge to hold long enough to finish the question.

It's fun to see your old home! Take lots of pictures! That's what she tells the girls. She puts them on their trains and airplanes and in charter vans for the last leg of their tour. She has herded them in Beijing, at the Great Wall and the Forbidden City, and in Xian to see the archaeological treasures. Here in Chengdu, she hustles them through the nature reserve, making sure that each girl who has paid her fifty dollars gets her picture taken standing next to an apathetic panda. Chengdu is where her duties end. She doesn't go to the orphanages with them; they are met on the other end by local guides who know the right people, who can make the introductions to the orphanage directors, and though she wouldn't go, no matter what they paid her, she wonders how much those local guides get tipped. A lot, she guesses, since the fatness of the envelope depends on the drop between the levels of a family's anxiety from the beginning of the trip to the end. She can always predict who will be the biggest tippers: they're the parents who arrive carrying their bodies stiffly, and as the days proceed, fill with relief like a belly swells with water. But she has her limits. She won't go to the orphanages and pretend to be delighted. One friend of hers, Rabbit, left Beijing to be a local guide in Hubei, and in another year or two, she'll be able to buy a car. In Beijing, owning a car would be a lot of trouble and expense, but if she had one, it would be blue like the one in the billboard on top of the apartment building where she lives with her parents. That color blue, with maybe a tinted window.

She won't be a local guide. And never, ever will she help them get the babies.

She hears a commotion. Hurrying down the path toward her are two guards and the parents. The missing boy, Sam, the guards clutch by his shirt between them. Daisy can see that one of the guards is very angry; he's yelling at the boy and jerking the shirt-sleeve he has bunched in his fist like a leash. The other guard is telling the angry guard to go easy. Sam isn't struggling but he isn't quite walking either; he's letting the guards pull him like a large piece of plastic tugged through the water, awkward to drag but not actively resisting. To Daisy's surprise, he isn't scared or embarrassed. He looks straight at her with an untroubled expression, which makes her think of the protesters she sometimes glimpses on her way past important government buildings who frustrate the soldiers by gazing at them patiently while being hauled away. He has the same dignity, unusual for a child.

"Let go of my son!" the mother is shouting. She's a wiry woman with the upper arm muscles of an acrobat; it looks to Daisy like she spends half her time standing on her hands. Since they came off the plane from Los Angeles in Beijing, this mother, call-me-JoJo, has worn shorts and sleeveless blouses and broad ugly sandals like paws attached to her ankles. She doesn't bother with a hat or umbrella but lets her face turn brown in the beating sun. Her husband, Huron, strides behind her. To Daisy he looks huge, nearly two meters, with alarming ears that seem to glow with pale whiteness. His eyebrows are white and most of his hair too, and he has a thick beard that started out clean and now looks dirty, stained by the air and the sweat of his exertions. His stomach hangs over the strap of his worn brown belt. He's too old to be a father. He hasn't been one of the tired ones though. He walks like a young man, purposeful and fast.

"We should lock him up!" yells the angry guard at Daisy. "He disturbed the animals! He dirtied their habitat!"

"Tell these men to get their hands off my son!" JoJo pleads. She looks like she's about to cry. The word *sob* pops into Daisy's head. It's one of her favorite words. Her best English teacher was from Leeds, England, and taught her *sob* along with *Spartan* and *vulpine*. Don't try these words on the Yanks, he warned her.

They have the vocabulary of an imbecilic oaf. He never slowed his speech like he was speaking to a child. Daisy had thought she was in love with him a little.

"I am sorry that the boy has caused you so much trouble," she says to the calmer guard. He lets go of the boy's shirt and stands back until the other guard lets go too.

"He should be locked up!" the angry guard repeats, but at least he isn't yelling and his fist has unclenched. JoJo grabs her son's shoulders and pulls him into her as though her breastbone will collapse into a cave where she could hide him.

"Miss," says the calm guard, addressing Daisy, "he behaved very badly. He climbed the fence and went into the red panda enclosure. Then he . . . ," the guard makes an ambiguous motion with his hands in front of his crotch. The father takes one step closer to the guards and frowns a question in Daisy's direction: What's the guard saying? What happened to his son?

"He pissed all over the plants!" said the angry guard. "It's a danger to the animals. He must be detained while I make my report."

"I apologize," says Daisy. She sees JoJo look toward the buses, but Daisy isn't going to hurry this transaction; it would only prompt the guard to do as he threatened. "This boy behaved very badly, but perhaps he didn't understand. He can't read the signs and didn't know he shouldn't cross into the animals' habitat. Then, being only a boy, he had to use the facilities but couldn't find any nearby. He is my responsibility." She's quiet for a moment, as though composing a solution. "I'll write a letter of apology to the director. And I'll make sure that I tell my boss to make clear to visitors that they cannot go past the fence."

The angry guard complains for another two minutes. Out of the corner of her eye, Daisy sees Huron put his hand on his back pocket, but when she doesn't move or look his way, he takes his hand away. This father isn't stupid. A bribe will get them into much bigger trouble. Finally the angry guard stops to take a breath.

"Arrogant Americans," he says to Daisy.

"What can you do," she shrugs to them both. "Most of them behave very well. Just once in a while, you get a bad one in the group." Still she doesn't move toward the buses until the guard turns and walks disgustedly away. The calm guard follows, and Daisy relaxes.

"I apologize for that," says Huron. "I gather my son did something objectionable."

Daisy doesn't answer but walks them silently back to the bus. Behind her, she hears JoJo pour out her own complaints to her husband. They climb on Bus A, and Daisy, on impulse, gets hurriedly off the bus and trots to Bus B, where she takes the front seat. She doesn't look back at Sam, though she knows he hopes she will. Is he sitting up front by himself, or did he find a seat near his parents? He won't go to the back with the girls. All week they've largely ignored him, once they realized that he was more interested in the places they're visiting than in them. Only his sister huddles with him at breakfast. She's fourteen, but she looks closer to Sam's age in her pink ruffled shirts and pink and white shoes. Most of the girls are twelve, thirteen, or fourteen, and most of them, like Sam's sister, Kate, are small for their ages, so they try to make up for it by wearing big hoop earrings and shiny oil on their lips or sticking in earphones and moving their hips to music that nobody else can hear. Sometimes one will have stuff on her toenails that looks like her foot got caught in a slamming door. *Bruise*, thinks Daisy. She can't help herself; she looks over at Bus A, and Sam waves to her, asking her to come back.

"Okay everybody?" Daisy calls over her shoulder.

"Is Sam okay?" the Bus B parents want to know. Some look annoyed that they've been kept waiting, though at least the bus is air-conditioned. Every day, they've complained about the weather. "I took three showers yesterday," one of the mothers boasted. Daisy perspires only a little. The umbrella helps and a cool state of mind and a light string bag; she can't understand why they carry so much with them.

"All okay," says Daisy. She tells the bus driver to take them back to the hotel. The story will get around the group fast enough, though she doubts that JoJo will include every detail. Daisy saw a wet patch at the front of the boy's shorts. Either he really had to go or he didn't have very good aim. She realizes now why she had to change buses. She's a little mad at the boy, behaving so badly. They had gotten to be friendly riding the bus together, and then, outside the panda house, they had had a conversation. She finds she is frowning and puts a hand to her forehead. It was a mistake to tell him what she did. He had asked her a question and, as he was just a child and she was speaking words in a language not her own, she found herself slipping almost by accident into the truth. He didn't say anything; he just took in her story. He's different from most of the other children she's met—a quiet thinker, serious, watchful. When he talks to his sister, he looks as shy as a suitor, listening to her closely, searching her face like a map. She's seen them eating together like a couple of newlyweds, whose careful attentions to one another's happiness might lead observers to the foolish assumption that they are somehow protected. She can tell he's devouring all the new things he's learning and judging for himself everything he sees. He had asked her yesterday, when they were flying to Chengdu, if he could skip the panda babies.

"It's weird that they're brought up in nurseries," he said. That surprised Daisy; most of the tourists wanted badly to see the babies. Some used to pay more so that they could cradle one in their arms until Western scientists interfered and put an end to the practice. She had reassured him that he didn't have to see the babies, and she had stayed outside with him while the rest of the group filed through. It was pleasant outside, cooler among the trees and with the cicadas for music. The sunlight didn't reach them through the afternoon haze, and the humid air felt thick and fertile. She liked the way it bathed and soothed her. They amused themselves by naming what they saw from the curving path, Sam pointing to light poles, benches, and trash cans, and Daisy supplying the words for him to learn. He imitated her perfectly. He played the clarinet, he told her. Saying the words was like playing musical notes. He taught her *clarinet*, and Daisy, relaxing, made the sound of that tricky word just like he did. He smiled once, showing big teeth like a beaver, and she had thought again, there's something about this boy. He was a nice change from all the hoop earrings and chatter. "Do you have any siblings?" he had asked, and that's when she had told him about her sister, maybe in a family, maybe dead.

I shouldn't have told him, the thought arises more firmly, and as it does, she admits to herself that she's been thinking that all along, the whole time that Sam was missing. I shouldn't have told him what my family never speaks of. A bad feeling expands in her chest as her dismay blossoms. She grabs a bottle of water and fumbles to get the cap off. The bus is lumbering through the heavy traffic. When they get to the hotel, she won't stop to give them instructions but will run upstairs and hide in her room until dinner. She could go to Sam and ask him not to tell—but there's no need. He won't have taken much notice of what she said. He's only a boy, interested in himself and not yet in the troubles of other people. Tomorrow he'll be leaving along with everyone else. If he cares about anything, he's thinking of his sister and of going with her tomorrow for her awful reunion visit.

Later, after they get back to the hotel and rest, the group gathers for the farewell dinner. Daisy passes out their tickets to the after-dinner show. She's seen it twenty times, performed by a large company of men and women in garish costumes, their faces painted like the imitation opera masks sold in the restaurant lobby, singing and dancing to canned music. The older girls in the group looked bored and embarrassed to be wearing the dresses that Daisy gave them this afternoon: red *qi pao* with side slits and tight collars that nobody wears anymore. You can't even buy one in the department stores. It's part of Daisy's job to pass out cultural mementos—postcards, tiny clay teapots, embroidered headbands, knotted bracelets. The red dresses were the final prize of the trip, but by then, exhausted and missing their friends back home, the girls didn't even look up when Daisy handed them out. Still, the girls have dutifully put on the dresses and now they stand together, all twenty-two of them, for a last group photograph before dinner. The other tourists point and whisper. *Orphans*, say their faces. *Gawk* is another good word, thinks Daisy.

"Daisy!" JoJo makes her way across the lobby, using both arms to push Sam in front of her like he was a baby carriage. This mother hasn't realized yet that her son is growing up. Daisy gave Sam an outfit too, and to her dismay, she sees that he's wearing it: dark blue pajamas with pants too short for his bamboo legs. She had not wanted him to have to dress up like a doll. He has his father's pale ears that stick out from his elegant head and a nose so little it hardly interrupts his face. His eyes are gray, which seems very strange to Daisy; she's seen blue and even green but never gray before. Like this afternoon, when he was being dragged along by the guards, he looks older than a boy, only this time, when she returns his steady look, she sees a little flicker of emotion. He's angry at his mother, is her impression. He has his own idea of what to say to Daisy.

"Sam has something to tell you," JoJo announces.

"I'm sorry," says Sam, not looking at his mother.

Daisy stares at him briefly. She would like to let him know that she's angry with him too—for making the group wait, for luring Daisy into answering all his questions—but more than that, she wants to erase their conversation.

"It's all right," she says, looking past him.

"Can Kate and I sit next to you at dinner?" he asks and rolls his eyes away from his mother. Daisy hesitates, but JoJo is watching. She thinks about the envelope that JoJo will hand her tomorrow.

"Okay, sure." She takes them to the table farthest away from the show. They are friendly again over dinner, laughing together at the awkward guide who lectured them on pandas. Daisy teaches Sam several new words, and Kate looks happy to be sitting with her brother, more relaxed in the darkened restaurant with the music blaring and their parents across the room than Daisy has seen her all week. When they get back to the hotel, their father thanks her for making the trip fun for his kids. Daisy hopes Huron and not JoJo will decide what goes in the envelope tomorrow.

But the good Sam is gone come the next morning, and the bad Sam makes trouble. Right after breakfast, he disappears again.

"He was here with Kate, making her a piece of toast because that's all she wanted, she was feeling queasy, and then he left the table to go back to the room and when we went back upstairs, he and his backpack were gone." That's what JoJo says in a strained, panicky voice.

"I'm sure he's all right," Daisy tells Huron briefly, and he says that he'll look outside near the hotel. Daisy rushes off to organize the other families into their traveling groups and to collect her envelopes and let them take her picture. She sends one group to the train station and another onto a charter bus. Now it's time to leave with the last group for the airport, but still Sam is missing.

"Kate," says Daisy, bending down to his sister. The girl looks very pale this morning, and she's not in pink but a thin white dress because she doesn't know that white is the color of mourning. "Did Sam tell you where he was going?"

Kate shakes her head. She's shivering in the air-conditioned lobby. Her collarbones jut above the collar of her dress like tiny shelves, empty and waiting. "I don't know where he is." She starts to cry, and her mother rushes over.

"What's wrong with him," she demands of her husband. "What the hell does he think he's accomplishing, like we're not going to finish it, having come all this way for vacation?"

Huron shakes his head. "I'll go look upstairs again."

"I'm sorry," says Daisy. She has called the Beijing office; they've given her instructions. "I have to take the other families to the airport. I'll come back after."

"You can't leave us here!" says JoJo, but Huron nods.

"I wish I had a goddamned cell phone," is all he says.

"We'll make other arrangements," Daisy tells him and glances at Kate. *Vacation* is what JoJo had called it. Most families don't call it that. *Affinity tour, heritage journey, roots trip, cultural awareness*—Daisy has learned all these new expressions. *A growing experience*—Daisy's heard that one too. She had to ask an American girl she knew in Beijing what that meant. Making your life bigger, the girl tried to explain. Well, when she gets back, she'll make their trip smaller. She expects Huron to tell her to book them a flight straight home.

Sam is sitting in the lobby when she returns. His father is beside him, heavy arms crossed. JoJo and Kate are upstairs, he reports. Sam had taken a taxi to a park in the city, but the taxi driver got nervous, not wanting to drop him off, a young kid with no Chinese and no parents, so he drove him back to the hotel with Sam protesting. He had evidently planned to spend a couple of hours; he had breakfast rolls in his backpack and a couple of bottles of water. Sam isn't looking so dignified anymore. His head is down; dried tears streak his face. His foot kicks the table leg and makes the ashtray jump.

"Stop that," says Daisy sharply in Chinese. Sam ignores her and kicks the table again. Huron doesn't come to his rescue the way his wife would but walks to the front desk to ask the clerk a question. It's Daisy's turn to stand guard over Sam. He'll run away again given half a chance.

"You're being a spoiled brat," she says in English. A good word, *brat*, it lands like a slap in the face.

Sam shrugs, kicking. "You don't want to go either. That's why you're not coming with us."

Daisy gapes at him. Yesterday's conversation rears again in her head, along with the unpleasant notion that what she told him is making him run away. What possessed her to entrust this boy with her secret? Loneliness, she fears, and the inkling of a feeling deep in her hollow heart that Sam would understand why it makes her sad and furiously angry that girls by the thousands are dumped for others to raise. A surge passes through her and leaves her shaking. She's sweated through her blouse; her body feels clammy in the chilly lobby. Her hair has fallen out of its neat bun, and she's so hungry, having been on the run all morning, that she'll have to dig in her suitcase for the spicy jerky she bought for her father. She's going to miss her flight unless she can get rid of them quickly. She wants to be done with this nuisance family; she should be heading home right now to her own mother and father. She leans down to speak to Sam tersely.

"You should listen to your parents. They do everything for you, bring you here, give you food and a home and lots of comforts. You owe them a lot so you should show it."

"You hate the orphanages," says Sam. "You said you hate that parents don't want their daughters. I don't want Kate to go. She's afraid of it, she doesn't want to go there, and my parents are making—"

Daisy interrupts him, practically shouting. "Your family is not my family. Kate has a mother and father. You are making problems for your sister, not being help to her, just getting into trouble." Her thoughts are crashing; she's furious with herself for saying the sentences badly. She leans closer to Sam, and as she does, she sweeps her eyes across the lobby. His father isn't looking, so she reaches over quickly and takes Sam's ugly ear between her thumb and forefinger. Whispers to him, "I have no sister," and twists his ear, hard, as an urgent warning. The boy is more

Chinese than she had guessed. He doesn't move and doesn't call out to his father. In his gray eyes, she sees his message: he hasn't told anyone. He never intended to tell.

Huron returns. He doesn't notice the boy's bright red ear. "Look," he says, "Sam screwed up and he knows it. I think I understand why, but right now, it doesn't matter. We need to change our flight and get going."

Daisy steps back and takes a deep breath. She doesn't look at Sam and tries to speak calmly. "I'll call the office," she says. "They can check the schedule and book you a flight home."

"We want to go on," Huron says. "To the orphanage, I mean."

It's a mistake, Daisy wants to tell him. Sam will run away again and Kate—. But instead of saying anything, Daisy finds a corner to make her call to Beijing.

"You have to take them there yourself," her boss tells her.

"I cannot. I cannot! It's not my fault they missed their flight. They have a stupid boy who ran off because his sister is unhappy. The kids don't want to go. The girl is practically having a breakdown. We should put them on a plane to go home tomorrow."

"No, I talked with the father. He insists they're going on and he wants you to take them. He'll pay for your ticket. This is the only solution. Since they missed their visit date, Rabbit is not available to take them anymore. She has an adoption group to lead in another city. Home office says you've got to take them."

No, thinks Daisy. She'll refuse to do it.

"My father is very sick," she says in a rush. "My mother called. He needs me right away. I'll make their arrangements and stay one more night here if I have to. Then I'll go home to Beijing and you can find them another tour guide."

"No one is available. You're the only one. I e-mailed Wisconsin. They say you have to do it."

Daisy throws her mobile into her bag and marches over to Sam and Huron.

"My boss says I have to take you." She spits out the words at Huron, raking him with her glare. She's learned something from all those agitating parents. "It's a lot of trouble, having to make new arrangements. Not only on this end, but on the other end too. There's no local guide. Your schedule must be corrected."

This time when Huron reaches toward his back pocket, she

makes sure he sees her staring at his wallet. The dirty green bills feel wonderfully soft in her hand.

They arrive late, almost midnight. She's called ahead to a hotel at the edge of the city. She makes them eat some snacks in the airport and checks them in, then goes to her own room and collapses. It's a local hotel in a smaller city, not like the fancy Western-style hotels where they've been staying up to now. She smiles thinly at the thought of JoJo studying the squat toilet in her dingy bathroom. She lies down on the bed, exhausted. The nylon coverlet on the bed reminds her of the hotel beds where she used to meet her lover, the English teacher who made her mouth sing. She went with him on weekend trips to small cities a day's rail ride from Beijing. Hotel clerks smirked when they saw her or made rude remarks that her teacher answered sharply. After sex, he didn't waste the language by naming parts of her body or declaring his love but made up little stories about a young Chinese girl who travels to England and makes hilarious blunders, asking for tea and spitting it out on the carpet because it was spoiled with milk and sugar. She knew he was leaving at the end of the school year. They bought dwarf melons from old men at the side of the road and sent round their curves a small, wicked blade that took off the peel like a net skimming the water. One afternoon, before they dozed together, she told him about her parents, how good they were to her. Her father, she said, went to America for research and might even have stayed, but he didn't want to abandon her. He came straight back, refusing his host's offer to take him to see Yellowstone or maybe the Grand Canyon. He had seen the state capitol building, he told her, and that was enough. He missed his family dearly.

"And I have a sister too," Daisy murmured. She was speaking to him in English. To speak in the other language let her push the story out.

Her lover lifted a strand of her hair and replaced it.

"In an orphanage?" he asked, fully understanding.

"Maybe," she said. "Perhaps when she was little. They never inquired. They left her on the steps of a police station in a small city they've never named for me." She rolled closer to his body. His hair was so thin, like grasshopper legs torn and collected. "And then they got me."

"Not the son they were holding out for."

She laid her head on the dry furze of his chest.

"Not the son, but by then, they were happy with a daughter. My mother was afraid she'd never have another baby. It took four years for her to get pregnant again. Even then, she couldn't nurse me." She added, in Chinese, "It was like the ghost of my older sister had sucked her dry completely," but she said it so quickly that she wasn't sure he understood her.

"They're lucky to have you," said her lover. His kindness drew a blanket of guilt over her heated body for having said aloud the family story, and she jerked to throw it off, jumping from the bed.

"Ding Xiu," he said, calling her by name. "Ding Xiu, Ding Xiu. It's all right. You don't need to worry." He drew her back and made love to her again. When they woke up later, he told her another story, this time about two girls who go to Leeds on a pilgrimage to learn how to make a decent pudding. She was laughing by the time he was finished. It's a good thing to talk to another person. But she should have done as he had and made up her story. To betray her parents' secret was to set down her swaddled sister and creep away again.

There's a knock at her door. It's JoJo, wrapped in one of Huron's sweat-stained shirts.

"Can I talk to you?" she asks.

Daisy frowns but lets her in, and JoJo takes the only chair so Daisy must perch on the edge of the hard bed, trying to keep from sliding off with the slippery nylon spread. She sees that JoJo is barefoot; doesn't she know to wear the hotel slippers? The woman looks frightened, clutching her husband's shirt.

"I'm very sorry about all this, Daisy."

Daisy sees her chance and treads carefully toward it.

"I'll get a driver to take you tomorrow. Then he'll drive you to the airport and you can go home from here. This is a much better way to travel, with the driver, yeah, and then straight to the airport. There's no good hotel in this city and it's not good to spend two nights in this one."

"What will it be like tomorrow? What should I tell Kate to expect?"

Daisy feels no duty to ease JoJo's worries. "I don't go to the orphanages," she answers shortly. She thinks of the panda nurseries, where the babies are raised by better than their mothers. No wonder Sam had refused to see them.

"But they don't speak any English, do they? The director and his staff? The children?"

Daisy shrugs. Rabbit has described for her the reunion visits. The smiling director, the polite exchange of gifts. A very old caregiver who may or may not truly remember giving that child a bottle. Some of the girls have fun, Rabbit has said, but some are so petrified they just stand there speechless.

"Kate asked to come," JoJo says. She is slumped in the chair and her voice is quiet. "Another girl in her school visited her orphanage last summer and came home and told Kate all about it. How fun it was to see her home country and then to go to the orphanage and put so many questions to rest. So Kate asked us if we would bring her. I don't know why Sam is so worried. He's not like this at home. He's very good to his sister. In fact, I think he feels guilty that we're his parents and Kate was adopted. You know how it is," she says, glancing at Daisy. "After you adopt, then you can get pregnant. Nature is funny. Second chance, second child."

Daisy puts out her hands to brace herself on the bed. It's airless in the room; she turned off the fan because it was too noisy. She's eaten nothing all day but beef jerky and crackers; she should try to stand up and splash some water on her face. She tries to think of a word in English because that always helps, it gives her focus, but nothing comes but rushing silence. The closeness rises up like a deadening noise around her, and the single overhead light seems to burst like a star in the air. A second later, she's doubled over, and JoJo is standing next to her, steady hand pushing Daisy's head between her knees.

"Breathe, breathe. That's it, more slowly. You poor thing. You haven't eaten all day." She reaches into her pocket and gives Daisy a bar of something sticky, which JoJo makes her eat in little bites.

"An energy bar," JoJo says. *Energy*, thinks Daisy, relieved that the words have returned. It helps to have her tongue divided.

"I'm ill," she tells JoJo.

"Then let's get you a doctor."

"No," says Daisy, "I just need to go home." She lies down on the bed, curled around the pillow. The light finds her and pricks at her like a needle. Her head aches, a drum that won't stop beating. If only she were home with her mother reading by the window and her father at the sink, carefully scrubbing their sandals clean.

JoJo touches Daisy's shoulder. "I don't know what we're so afraid of," she says. "Our feelings, I suppose, more than the situation." She tugs a knot into her husband's shirttails so she looks like a teenager, sporty at one in the morning. "You go on home. We'll be fine tomorrow." She walks to the bathroom, flips the switch, and pulls the door toward her, leaving a sliver of light. Then she turns off the light in Daisy's bedroom. Daisy closes her eyes, grateful. In the sanctified room, her family's story bleeds into the darkness, and its end, unfinished, pains her a little less. JoJo's voice floats above her.

"Sam—," she says. "It's probably best if he doesn't see you in the morning. I'll tell him you had to go home and said you wished us a safe and pleasant journey." The door clicks shut as JoJo leaves her. Sleep evens her back into a single language so her mind stops its drumming and takes its ease for the first time in many days. She dreams of her sister walking with a playmate down a street in the unnamed city, though it's not a dream that fills her but the early morning images that visit upon waking. Maybe her sister grew up and went out into the world. Maybe she has a family now who knows the whole of her story. She had told Sam that she was afraid, if she went to the orphanages, that she would start looking for her sister and never stop, but this is another way to look for her sister, in her imagination, with the dawn seeping in. She climbs from the bed and takes a long drink of water, then steps quietly from the room and walks down the hall to where Sam and Kate are sleeping. She waits patiently until seven o'clock in the morning. The door opens slowly. It is Sam, with his backpack, ready to bolt again.

"Sam," she says. She takes his elbow. "Don't leave. Your sister needs you."

Sam pulls back without breaking her grasp on his arm. She can feel him nervous and defiant in her fingers. She asks herself what JoJo would do to soothe him, or what her own mother does to calm her daughter. She doesn't know how to be a proper mother; she drops her hand and speaks to him brusquely.

"It should be easy, just walking around and talking. Your parents will take care of her. Your mother will know what to do." She sees Sam jerk down his stiffened shoulders. He hunches them up again and looks straight at her.

"I want you to come with us," he says. His voice is clear though his mouth seems to be trembling. Gray eyes, she thinks, look less than strange this morning. She hears a door open down the hallway behind her. Sam doesn't look but keeps his gaze level. A person approaches, maybe Huron, maybe JoJo. Her heartbeat quickens, racing forward before she is ready. *I can't*, her mind is saying, but she knows with sudden certainty that she won't be running. The moment, the boy, the family have seized her, demanding her attention, twisting her hard to keep her here this morning. There is no way that she can stop it. She closes her eyes to foretell the next hour. They'll meet in the lobby after breakfast, Sam's hand gripping his father's, and JoJo hurrying, clasping an umbrella that she'll use to keep the hot sun from her daughter's face. Kate, in pink, will trail behind her mother, who will turn every third step to give Kate an encouraging smile. Daisy will be waiting for them. In her bag, she'll have packed bottles of cold water and a map of this strange, new city.

"Take a picture of us," she'll say and put her arm about Kate's shoulders. Kate will be quivering, afraid and excited. "Let's go," Daisy will tell her. As soon as she opens her eyes, this will happen. She'll lead the family out to where the dull sun hovers. As soon as she can, her eyes will open, and they'll all walk together into the nourishing heat.

The
Scottish
Play

I am making straight for my table by the window to eat when whom should I see in line behind me but Mrs. Liang, the other Chinese lady, who never used to come on Thursdays but now here she is. "Good afternoon, Mrs. Liang," I say very nicely, "would you like to join me for lunch?" She nods, also nicely, and I point out my table, which is still completely empty since most of the others who come for lunch on Thursdays know that I am always the first one to sit at the table by the window. Ronnie sits there too, and Gloria, who is ridiculously deaf so you don't have to bother trying to include her in the conversation. Mr. Murphy sits there once in a while; he's an Irishman but I don't think he drinks because his nose looks very young though he's eighty-two years old and the rest of him is spotted. There's another man in a wheelchair; the helpers at Little House put him at my table because they know I will wave them over if he spills too much food on himself. He can't say much but it doesn't matter because I can speak for him which some of the others don't do, maybe they are too embarrassed or think it's none of their business, the well-being of others. I took care of my husband for fifty years before he passed last year. The helpers at Little House remember Cecil well. "He was a nice man," they tell me often, when I ask them for a second dessert because the Little House chocolate pudding was Cecil's favorite. "You have to wait until everyone has been served," the young ones tell me, but the older workers bring me the second dessert when they come to pour our water. Cecil would want me to invite Mrs. Liang to join me, which I don't mind doing so long as she doesn't mention her grandson.

Mrs. Liang sets down her tray and I see right away that she's put on weight around the middle. She's wearing a crocheted sweater that bulges like a money belt under its lumpy surface, this lady who used to dress like she was too good for the rest of us. Her husband Joe is gone so maybe she reaches for any old thing in her closet, though back when we had husbands her old things were always nicer than my best. Joe had money from a Hong Kong connection; Cecil said it wasn't gangster money and that I should curb my wild imagination, though truth be told, I always made him laugh because I showed him exactly what I meant whenever I told him a story: a cold-blooded gangster crouching in a doorway, a drunken cook who was chasing a squawky chicken, a rich lady, head down, hurrying to the abortionist because her lover's wife had gotten reports in America and was coming back home to check up on her husband. Everything Cecil had he earned by hard work and investments. He never asked his family for anything he didn't deserve. When I played the rich lady, I put my nose straight up in the air and didn't look to my left or my right. Ha ha, Cecil said, for a plain good woman, you know how the other half lives. Once we got to America, we didn't have servants anymore.

"You look very nice today," I say to Mrs. Liang. I am speaking in English, which I speak very well because I learned it young, the way you're supposed to, at Miss Allingham's School in Shanghai.

Mrs. Liang speaks it too, almost as well as I do, but her Chinese is full of peculiar expressions that only those people from the countryside say. Anyway, both of us are so used to English by now. We never had to ask our children to translate.

"Thank you," she replies, smoothing that lumpy sweater when any other lady would protest and joke that she has gotten fat. This is always the way with this particular lady. I won't say she brags about her money like Mrs. Chow's sister—what a hotshot she thinks she is, making a big show after dinner of taking her toothpicks out of a gold-plated case; you'd think they were made of ivory the way she holds them daintily with the tips of her fingers as though they weren't used for digging pork shreds from her teeth—but Mrs. Liang has little ways of setting herself apart. Joe wasn't like that. Cecil liked Joe; they used to go to the racetrack together, and Joe said Cecil brought him good luck though Joe lost money while most of the time Cecil was winning. So that's what I mean by Cecil's investments. He bought Janny's bedroom set with his winnings one year, white canopy bed with hearts and flowers.

"I'm surprised to see you here," I say. On Thursdays, lunch at Little House is only three seventy-five. The Sigal Foundation gave a two-year grant to subsidize Thursdays, and that's a very nice way to spend your money, not wasted on dusty museums or lazy heirs but given straight to the people who count their pennies every week. On Mondays, Tuesdays, Wednesdays, they charge the full six dollars. "Don't you usually come on Mondays, Tuesdays, or Wednesdays?"

Mrs. Liang nods. "I don't like the food they serve on Thursdays," she says.

Well, that takes the cake, because her tray is piled high with macaroni pasta and two pieces of bread and two pats of dairy spread.

"Really?" I say, staring at her plate. "Cecil and I always liked Thursdays the best. The other days, the menu never changes, but on Thursdays the chef always makes a nice surprise." There is no Friday, so Thursdays, it's true, they use what's left over.

"Joe always said Cecil was a natural born gambler." Mrs. Liang sticks her fork into her mound of pasta and carries a load to her mouth. My mouth drops open just like hers. What have I done to deserve such rudeness other than invite this lonely lady to share my table by the window? She's acting like a peasant who will trample her neighbor to grab the sweetest melon.

"It's too bad that your husband didn't have my husband's good fortune," I say. "It wasn't Joe's fault that he lost so often; he was a smart man, everybody knows. Probably the ancestors are restless spirits, not buried well or burdened by family shame."

"Oh, in America we don't worry about such things as ghosts and evil spirits and all that old-fashioned nonsense." A lie, I know it, because Joe is buried in the best section of Mesa Verde where all the Chinese want to go because the feng shui is ideal. I tried to buy a plot there for Cecil and me; all full, they told me, and then six months later Joe Liang went right in.

"Ha ha," I say. "I don't have the nerve to offend the ancestors like you. I may be American but I am still Chinese."

"America doesn't want you if you don't want to be like them. Look what's happening to immigrants these days. All those fences they're building at the borders. Joe always told Norman: you have to join in and beat the other fellow, that's how you find out what good you are for this life. Now, Norman"—that's her son, a well-mannered boy; he takes after his father—"he never felt that he was at any kind of disadvantage. He didn't complain that the world didn't treat him right. Did I tell you that his son, the one who went to Stanford, is now a navy SEAL? That's the most elite kind of American soldier."

Here we go, the grandson, and I'm not even through with my soup.

"That's very nice for you, having a grandson who will get the chance to travel. He can send you postcards from deserts all over the world. My granddaughter, Amy, she might go to Canada this summer. Have you ever been to Canada? Cecil and I saw the Rockies there one year." I have the good taste not to mention that Amy will soon be the lead in her high school play.

Mrs. Liang sets down her fork for the first time since we started. She puts the corner of her napkin to her eye. "Joe always wanted to see the Canadian Rockies. He loved to ride the train. He said it would be nice to go by train in the summer."

We finish our soup and the macaroni pasta.

"You and Joe got to go back to China."

"Six times," says Mrs. Liang. "And now there's a scholarship at Joe's old high school."

"I hear that Shanghai looks nothing like it used to."

"It looks like *Star Wars*. All tall buildings with tops like rockets."

I know what she's talking about. Amy and I watched the DVDs together. Amy would make a good Chinese Princess Leia. "Miss Allingham's School is probably not there anymore," I say.

Mrs. Liang nods. "Old things have to make way for the new."

Suddenly I give a little chuckle. Mrs. Liang looks at me, laughing a little too. "We're hot now," I tell her. "All the young people want to go to China!"

"Under globalization, it's cool to be Chinese!"

"So you're Chinese?" says Ronnie, the other lady who sits at the window table. She sits down and takes everything off her tray, the way she does, first the soup, then the plate of pasta, the bread, the fruit cup, the plastic glass for water. She pushes her tray into the middle of the table where there isn't enough room, and Mrs. Liang and I have to pull our trays closer. "I thought you were Korean! Isn't it silly, I didn't want to ask, because my late husband's brother fought in the war against the Koreans, not that it matters, it was all so long ago. He came home changed but the family kept quiet. Anyway, all these Thursday lunches, and here I was, thinking you were Korean, when in fact, you're Chinese, and the Chinese were on our side in one of the wars, weren't they? Besides, things change, countries do too, and you speak such good English that it's easy to talk to you. I don't understand these people who won't learn English, like the girls at the nail parlor who do my manicures. Why bother to come here at all?"

I glance at Mrs. Liang. She is staring at Ronnie's hands; then she looks up at me and raises her eyebrows. Yes, she is right; I never noticed before what ugly hands Ronnie has, the skin so dry it looks like her knuckles have dandruff, and with red painted nails that look foolish on such an old witch.

"This is my good friend, Mrs. Liang," I tell Ronnie. "I'm very happy to see her. Our husbands were old friends who shared many of the same interests. From now on, if she comes on a Thursday, I'll be saving a seat for Mrs. Liang by the window."

"What about Gloria?" Ronnie cranes her neck, looking for her friend Gloria, who isn't here today, or maybe she's figured out that Ronnie isn't worth her time, not that it matters to Gloria, who's so deaf that that's probably the reason she puts up with Ronnie; she can't hear a word of what Ronnie has to say.

"She's at another table," I say, and I watch Ronnie twitch her woodpecker head in all directions looking for Gloria. A lady her age shouldn't pile her hair like that.

"Well, I'm not giving up my seat at this table," Ronnie says. "I like the window and it's been my seat forever."

"I've been thinking about switching to Mondays anyway," I say. "I hear the food's better on Mondays. Fresher food is nicer, don't you think?"

"They do a nice navy bean soup on Mondays," Mrs. Liang says. We make a plan to come for lunch on Monday next week.

———

It doesn't last very long, this warm and friendly feeling between Mrs. Liang and me. Before the navy bean soup has left the ladle, she starts telling me about how she's remodeling her kitchen. "I want to update the condo in case my son has to sell it." It's bad luck to worry aloud about when you might pass over. They live at the top of the hill near the duck pond. Mrs. Chow told me that they overpaid for the condo, yet here is Mrs. Liang putting in granite countertops and a stacked washer and dryer. Cecil and I used to own a house but now I live with my daughter, Janny. Not a day goes by that I don't dream that I still have the house. I wouldn't change a thing about it, no new countertops, no stacked washer and dryer, just live in it like before with my old pots and pans and the doorbell that sounded like a church chime.

"But you're so lucky," Mrs. Liang interrupts my dreaming, "that you have a daughter who is willing to take you in. My daughter-in-law said that I could have their spare bedroom, but I said no. I'd have to give up so much of my independence."

"Oh," I say innocently, "Mrs. Liang, did you finally learn how to drive?"

"Drive, who needs to drive? The Rediwheels bus picks me up right at my front door and takes me wherever I need to go—the doctor's, the store, the public library. Right here to Little House for navy bean soup." She slurps a big spoonful with too much en- thusiasm, and smashed navy bean drops onto her blouse, so now I can see how come her clothes don't look like they used to. Where is her son, that he isn't looking after his mother? A new washer and dryer won't do the laundry for you.

"In China, we always had a driver." I'm not a bad driver, only one fender bender in the past six months, not my fault: he was talking on his cell phone and stopped very fast when he should have kept moving.

"My grandson, Michael, he likes to drive me too. 'Where shall we go today?' he asks me. He took me to see the Stanford campus before he became a navy SEAL."

"I don't take every meal with my daughter and her husband." What's a seal? Her grandson belongs in a zoo, not the army. "Most of the time, I eat an earlier supper, and on Thursdays I drive my- self here." Janny and her husband both work at their kitchen table. Freelance, they call it, but they pay all their taxes just as if they had a boss. I don't want to live with you, I told Janny directly, but she's very pious and she and her husband insisted and I had to sell the house to pay taxes of my own.

"Which part of the house is yours?" Mrs. Liang asks me just when one of the young ones comes over to clear away our trays. As her tray sails off, Mrs. Liang leans over to grab at a roll but she misses. The young one frowns and gives her mine, which I only nibbled.

"I live downstairs, not anywhere near my daughter. It's a three- bedroom house. Very big, lots of sliders." Mrs. Liang made sure to tell me that she was replacing her back door with sliders.

Mrs. Liang nods knowingly. "It's not so good to sleep near your married daughter." She's taking aim at me the way she swiped at her hard roll. She has her grandson but Janny has only a daughter.

"That Mrs. Liang!" I fume to my daughter, Janny. "If Joe hadn't been such a good friend to Cecil, I wouldn't give her the time of day!" Two or three times, Joe loaned Cecil money when some of Cecil's investments didn't turn out the way he expected. Cecil offered to pay him interest, but Joe wouldn't take it. I'll bring them my orange cake, I promised Cecil, though it pained me to think of standing at their front door with my head bowed down and a cake heavy in my hands, and then I didn't do it because Joe told me his wife wouldn't eat it, she was always watching her weight. Cecil was mad at me, but I said, Joe told me not to, and then he stopped fretting and went back to his job at the restaurant. He always intended to repay Joe one day.

"'All brand-new granite counters,'" I say, puffing out my cheeks and sticking out my stomach to look like the new Mrs. Liang. I show Janny how she slurps when she's eating navy bean soup. I can capture Mrs. Liang's exact expression because my nose has grown wider now that my hair is so thin.

Janny peers up from the kitchen table. All day long she hunches at her laptop computer. Why couldn't she be a pretty girl like I was? When I was Janny's age and even after I was married, there were men who liked to look me over. Joe Liang, he looked at me more than once, though Mrs. Liang pretended not to notice. Janny's voice is soft and uncertain; she makes me think of a factory worker drowned out by the noise of machinery. I worked as a seamstress, just for a little while, and then Joe loaned Cecil a few extra dollars so I could quit and take proper care of my daughter.

"She's lonely," says Janny. "Uncle Joe's only been gone since October."

"She's always going on about making changes and you better keep up with the times but she's the one who is so old-fashioned! She thinks having a grandson is better than Amy! Amy, Amy!" I call to my granddaughter.

"Don't," begs Janny. "I just got her to sit down and finally do her homework."

"Just five minutes, how is that any bother?"

Amy runs into the kitchen to give me a hug. She's eighteen years old, as beautiful a girl as you would see in the movies. I can't believe it, she's almost six feet tall; it must be her father, the tallest Chinese in his class. He was good at basketball and then he married Janny. Joe gave his approval the first time they were introduced. He'd make a good son-in-law, he told Cecil, and that was enough to make Cecil give his consent. Why is she even asking? I said to Cecil, disgusted. A modern girl doesn't need her father's permission! Amy takes after me. She's not anything like her mother. She looks you right in the eye and laughs out loud when she wants to.

"Granny, guess what? I got a callback for the lead in the play!"

"That's wonderful!" I grab my girl by her slender waist, and we skip around the kitchen, knocking the back of Janny's chair.

"Be careful with Granny! She can't afford a fall!"

I ignore Janny and skip a little harder.

"I mean, a fall might break her hip," explains Janny weakly.

"Money, money, money, money," sings Amy. It's from a pop song, I think. Amy, like me, gets tired of such talk. "I like being with you, Granny," she says to me, squeezing. "You never worry like my mom does all the time." And then she hunches and shivers in exact imitation of Janny, so I do it too until we both are screeching.

"Out damnéd spot! Out, I say!" I lift my hand to examine it in the kitchen and turn to chide Janny. "You said she wouldn't get it. You said the teacher wouldn't choose a Chinese for the best part."

"Mom doesn't want me to be in the play," says Amy, tossing her long black hair. The front is cut with a razor so there are strands that cup her face, like an artist has outlined her, the central figure in the palace courtyard, the one you're supposed to notice enjoying her riches. You'd never see that in a real Chinese painting. It's never a woman who's got that kind of money. But Cecil's happy on the other side so I know he'll pave Amy's path with gold.

"Your schoolwork suffers when you don't pay attention," says Janny, but the way her eyes slide you can tell she knows that it's too late to forbid it, and when has she ever said no to Amy? Amy and I have been practicing the part for weeks, memorizing the lines and studying up on the story. We know it's bad luck to say the name of the play out loud; it's an old acting tradition because saying the name brings you bad fortune. I'm sure that the teacher is going to pick Amy. "All the perfumes of Arabia will not sweeten this little hand. Oh, oh, oh!" I know the play well; we did a production at Miss Allingham's School my last year there, before the war began, and even though I didn't get to play the Lady, I played the Gentlewoman who tells exactly what she has seen—

her boss, the Lady, reliving murder in her sleep. I've been showing Amy how to wash her hands in the air before her, and we stride the upstairs hallway, "Fie, my lord, fie!" Amy makes a magnificent Lady with her hair swinging wildly down by her face and her black eyes gleaming. "What hath quenched them hath given me fire!" she growls. I will sew her a red gown with bell sleeves and lace. Wait till I tell Mrs. Liang that my granddaughter Amy is going to play the lead.

But Mrs. Liang won't let me tell her about Amy. All she wants to talk about is her grandson, Michael.

"SEAL," she explains, "that stands for Sea, Air, Land. They get sent on the most important missions." She uses the word *elite* again, though she doesn't know how to pronounce it. Ee-light. Her son would be embarrassed to hear her get it wrong. I never embarrass Janny, because when I make a mistake my confidence always saves me. I want Amy to learn that from me.

"What did Joe have to say? When his only grandson volunteered to become a soldier?" Joe and Cecil were soldiers in China until they got away one night like all the smart ones did. That's how they met, going under the wire. Another one was shot but not Joe or Cecil, and after they got away, nobody came looking. They went back home to school until they got to this country. Joe knew exactly how bad the army is.

Mrs. Liang doesn't have an answer. She looks away and pretends she didn't hear me. Her spoon doesn't dive down into her rice pudding. Ah ha, I think, so Joe wasn't happy. Love your new country but no need to sign up to be killed.

"All wars are bad," I say. "The government always lies to the people. You and I know that. But young people, they don't listen to us. Joe knew it was better to take care of your family first."

Mrs. Liang looks down at her soup bowl. I see her hands disappear under the table. "I guess he leaves the country tomorrow. My son called to tell me. I sent my grandson a letter. I should have mailed it sooner. I don't think he's gotten it yet." She blows her nose into her scratchy napkin. We are quiet together. She's thinking, as I am, about what we remember. So many countries put their boots on China—the Japanese, British, Americans, French, and Germans, and then the Communists, who took everything left over. I should be used to losing houses. Mrs. Liang sighs and puts her hands back on the table. She doesn't want to talk about her grandson anymore.

"How is your granddaughter, Amy?" she asks. So I tell her about how Amy got the callback for the lead. "I won't say the name of the play out loud; that's bad luck, all actors know it. It's by William Shakespeare, about a man who murders the king so he can take over the throne."

She shrugs, unimpressed. "Most of the plays fit that description."

Maybe she thinks she knows more Shakespeare than I do, but she didn't go to Miss Allingham's School in Shanghai.

"There are three witches." I hold my spoon in my fist, stick it straight down into the navy bean soup, and start chanting with a cackle.

"Oh, you mean *Macbeth*," says Mrs. Liang.

I glare at her. "Don't say the name! It brings ill fortune!"

Mrs. Liang laughs. "I don't remember that Cecil was superstitious. In fact, Joe told me that Cecil was a very smart gambler. If he had chosen to go into business, he could have done well for himself. He played the odds, not the omens."

She's very clever. I can hardly argue that Cecil wasn't smart.

"Besides," says Mrs. Liang, "the curse of *Macbeth* only happens if you say the name of the play inside the theater. That's when actors call it 'The Scottish Play.' Otherwise, it's perfectly all right to say it."

She's wrong, of course, but I'm too polite to correct her. I tell her not to worry because I'm sure that the teacher will give Amy the part. Later, I light an extra stick of incense, one for Amy and one for Michael Liang. His grandmother won't do it so somebody better.

Mrs. Liang doesn't come for lunch the next Monday. I think about going to Little House on Thursday, but I walk to the park instead and eat my sandwich on a bench in the sun. Ronnie and

Gloria will have filled up the table by now, and I don't want to go if I can't sit by the window. Vitamin D makes your fingernails stronger, or is that E—I get the two mixed up. A mother sits down with a little boy in a stroller. I tug the boy's hat down more firmly over his ears, and the mother jumps up like I've rubbed against his privates. "I guess it is kind of windy," she says when I give her my look, and I point out how the boy's nose is already dripping. Then I'm sorry I've done it because she hurries him into the car, and I finish my lunch with only the birds to talk to. My own nose is dripping so I swipe it with my handkerchief which I squeeze into a ball, thinking about Amy and how I must look. Does Amy see me the same way that mother did? I probably looked old to her, being all bundled up in my padded blue jacket and wearing a knit cap like her son's pulled over my head, but Amy knows how well I skip in the kitchen and knows I can memorize as much and as fast as she can. She's learned all of her lines and I've learned some of the man's part so I can cue her, though I'd rather be the Lady than the King. He needs to be pushed to get anything accomplished, but his wife was strong until she went crazy. I had to push Cecil to go to Joe for the money. He didn't want to; he was ashamed, he said. You saved him from the army, I had to remind my husband, and it was true; he showed Joe how to roll down the hill after dark and where the two of them could dive under the wire. Joe was happy to help Cecil whenever he asked. I'm sure Joe never mentioned anything to his wife; he knew she wasn't happy when he looked me over, so why bring up the fact that he had loaned Cecil and me money? They had so much extra, there was no point in telling. Sometimes when I'm talking to Mrs. Liang, I feel like she's staring at me and thinking about the money, but then we go on and the subject isn't mentioned. She's putting in granite countertops; she's stacking her washer and dryer, and even after that, Mrs. Chow assures me, Mrs. Liang will have a lot left over. He wasn't very good at the racetrack, but I guess Joe Liang was lucky enough where it counted.

"You better let me take you to the doctor," says Janny, bringing me a cup of boiling hot water.

"I'm not sick!" My head aches and my chest is hurting but I won't go unless they drag me. I've had words with that man at the Urgent Care window. Say "Medi-Cal" to him and his brown face blackens.

"You should have stayed home for lunch, not sat in the park all alone."

I glare at Janny but for once she doesn't back down.

"You have no office! You work at the kitchen table! I don't want to bother you when you are tap-tapping."

"You said you were going to Little House," says Janny. "I thought Aunt Heidi was meeting you there today."

"Everybody else, when we got to America, we chose American names," I call to Amy out in the hallway. "Your grandfather chose Cecil. I picked Mildred. That foolish old lady thinks she's from the Swiss Alps. Don't come in to hug me! Keep away so you don't catch my cold."

Amy ignores me and bounds into the room outstretched.

"Stop!" I command her. She drops on the bed, laughing, and hugs my feet instead.

"Your feet feel like corn husks," she says, lifting them lightly.

"I'll bring bad luck," I tell her, frowning. "Go light the incense while we wait." She brings me the telephone and sets it on my bed. If she got the part, the teacher will call her.

"You talk to her, Granny. I want it too badly."

I beam at her mother and lie back like a queen on my pillow. When did Janny ever want something so much?

"If you're not better tomorrow, I'm taking you to the doctor," says Janny.

I try to sit up to answer but my head doesn't raise itself quickly. I don't like this Janny who's speaking like that to her mother. She's out the door before I can chide her. Mrs. Chow warned me about this very problem: how the children get bossy when they think we are dying. Or if we're not dying, we're sick or getting older. She has a daughter who always did what she told her; then Mr. Chow passed, and the daughter took control. Mrs. Chow will have to move to Philadelphia where the daughter is a teacher and the house is very small. Is Janny going to change like that and try to take over? I sink my head back into the worn-out pillow.

"Aunt Heidi is right, you know," says Amy. "You only say 'The Scottish Play' when you're inside the theater."

"Why make a bad bet when it's just as easy not to?" Michael Liang, for instance. He didn't have to put up his hand and go.

The telephone rings. I snatch to my ear.

"Amy!" I am calling. "You got the part! You got the part of the Lady!" I clap my hands as my girl dances. She will have to go mad and that might tempt the spirits, but before that happens she'll wear a crown on her head.

I call Mrs. Chow. Where is Mrs. Liang? She's not showing up for lunch on Mondays. I went four times and didn't see her. I called her house but she didn't answer. It's not good news, Mrs. Chow tells me. Mrs. Liang isn't so happy. She misses Joe and worries about her grandson. From the day he left the country, she hasn't been able to sleep. She canceled the granite countertops and didn't stack her washer and dryer. Her son, Norman, has had to hire a lady to go over twice a week to cook food and make sure that Mrs. Liang washes.

"Are you sure?" I ask Mrs. Chow. "The last time I saw her, Mrs. Liang was eating. She told me that Rediwheels does all her driving for her."

"Norman wants her friends to go over to cheer her up."

I don't make any promise. After all, I told Mrs. Liang that Amy was going to get the lead part, and now look, Mrs. Liang won't leave her condo. She's jealous of me having such a beautiful granddaughter. She doesn't deserve to see Amy up onstage.

But tonight the play opens, and I have an extra ticket and I think of Mrs. Liang. It's been two months since we last had lunch together; wouldn't it be good of me to be nice to an old friend? Cecil would want me to treat Joe's wife well. Watching Amy would make anybody happy; she's so good in the part—her teacher has said so—and even Janny is excited, fussing over Amy's costumes and going early to run the concession stand. Mrs. Liang shouldn't miss such a special occasion. There's no need to call her; I'll make a nice surprise.

"Mrs. Liang!" I call as I knock on the front door, hard. She doesn't have a bell that sounds like a church chime. "It's me, Mildred, come to take you out!"

Mrs. Liang opens the door, and I have to peer in to see her. It's a sunny spring day but her entryway is dark, and the drapes in the living room are closed tight over the windows. Mrs. Liang is a strange powdery color, as though she's been standing under a forsythia and the yellow dust has drifted down and settled all over her face. She's no longer fat but thin and wasted, and she's wearing a shirt that looks like one of Joe's. The sleeves are rolled up so I see her wrists and her cramped fingers, like little scrubbing brushes stuck on the ends of a stick. There is an undersmell in the house of nasty garbage and over that, the fresh cooking of a meat dish or two.

"Mrs. Liang!" I exclaim. I don't want to touch her. "I came by to see you. How are you doing?"

A figure appears behind her, and I almost back away because I think that it's Joe, returned to haunt his wife.

"Auntie Mildred!" says Norman. The expression on his face is so full of relief that I remember him as a boy, always glad to see Cecil, who took him to the racetrack and let him bet on ponies. "Mom," says Norman. "Here is Mildred; say hello, say hello!"

Mrs. Liang does as he asks and then shuffles to the living room and sits down in Joe's leather chair. There are dishes scattered on the floor near her feet and shredded Kleenex and a sanitary napkin, curled on its side like a fish.

"How are you, Auntie Mildred? I'm sorry I haven't called you for a while. I've been a little busy holding down the fort." Norman looks at me helplessly and wraps the dishtowel he's been holding around his right hand tightly.

"I came over to see if your mother would come out with me. I have an extra ticket to Amy's play this evening."

"Amy's play, Mother," says Norman. He leans over to touch her shoulder. "How nice of Auntie Mildred! Let's help you get dressed." He hurries into the kitchen to leave the towel, then shepherds his mother into her bedroom. I think he'll call me in to dress her, but he doesn't; instead, I wait for the longest time while I hear him persuading her to put on other clothes and brush her hair and use the toilet. When they come out of the bedroom, Mrs. Liang looks better. She says hello and meets my smile though she hasn't let go of Norman.

"Here we go, Mother." Norman unpeels her and hands her off while he drapes a sweater over her shoulders. "Thank you, Auntie Mildred," he whispers into my ear. I lead Mrs. Liang down the sidewalk to my car and look back once to see Norman go inside. He has four hours to clean his mother's condo, and I know he'll get it spotless because he doesn't know what else to do.

I park the car and take Mrs. Liang into the auditorium. She says she's okay and manages a smile. Other than that, she doesn't speak, and I think I better not ask about the condo or lunch dates or her grandson, Michael. I hope she's not going to try anything funny like stand up in the middle and run out, crying. Shakespeare can have that effect on people. I once saw a grown man sob with his head in his hands. I'm a little bit sorry I brought her tonight, but then I remember the relief on Norman's face and think, he's right, Amy will do her good.

Trumpets blare, and the play begins. The witches stir and plot and huddle. They give their warnings along with their predictions but the gods never want us to heed what we already know. My girl walks on alone to read her husband's letter and scorns the milk of human kindness. I almost can't watch her, so fine she looks up onstage. I have to hold my breath like I'm swimming underwater because I know every line as well as she does and might forget myself and speak them out for her. At intermission, Mrs. Liang doesn't have a word of praise for Amy but complains that the seat is awfully hard and she can't see well and can't hear much either. She asks me to take her to the bathroom. I crane to look for Janny but she's already outside, selling Coca-Colas. It's going to be crowded; we might not make it back to our seats in time, and I'm afraid to get up and disturb the way things are going, everything perfect, and Amy flawless. I tell Mrs. Liang to go find it herself, and she gets up and goes, good riddance.

Mrs. Liang doesn't return. She doesn't see Amy wash her hands in the air or the King cut down after the soldiers' final battle. I don't budge from my seat when the theater empties; I'm imagining what it feels like to stand on the stage and bow.

"Take me home," says a voice, angry and tired. Mrs. Liang is blocking the aisle. Her hair is messed and her sweater is missing.

"I want to see my granddaughter. Then we can go."

"I couldn't get back in. They closed the doors and I didn't know what to do. I sat outside waiting for you to come get me."

I hear people clapping outside the doors; the actors must be meeting their parents and friends in the hallway. I stand up to go to Amy. Mrs. Liang pokes me with the edge of her pocketbook.

"I want to go home. You've got to take me. You'll see her later. You get to see her every day."

"Yes, that's right. I live with my daughter. I don't have money like you do. But you have to wait until I talk to Amy."

"Take me home, now."

"In ten minutes." I wish I'd brought flowers like some of the other parents.

"You owe us money," says Mrs. Liang. "You and your husband. Joe and I want our money back." She might be yelling at me from the front of the stage, so loud are the words she's shouting.

But she's the one who always talks about putting the past behind us. "Joe is dead. He doesn't need the money. Cecil offered to pay it back many times, and Joe always told him that friends don't keep track."

"Liar," Mrs. Liang says. Her dull eyes have taken on life again.

"Scrooge," I say. She thinks she knows Shakespeare, does she know Dickens?

"Macbeth," says Mrs. Liang. "Macbeth, Macbeth, Macbeth."

"Shut up. You're not allowed to say it. Get out of here if you're going to talk like that."

"Macbeth, Macbeth, Macbeth." Each time she says it, she jabs me hard with her pocketbook until I'm twisting it out of her hand like a ninja and we're both shoving and shouting.

"Granny!" calls Amy. She skips across the stage straight toward me, the way we skip in the dingy kitchen. With a final shove of the pocketbook I turn, just in time to see my girl topple.

———————————

I don't see her anymore for lunch on Mondays. She never apologized for Amy's broken ankle, and I never wrote her after Michael was killed. I wrote to Norman but not to his mother. I read in the newspaper about the Medal of Honor. He threw himself on a grenade to protect his comrades. Oh no, I might have joked to Mrs. Chow had she not moved away to live with her bossy daughter. Another thing for Mrs. Liang to boast of. But I didn't make the joke. I only felt sorry.

I mean to go back to Little House on Thursdays. When the weather gets cold again and I can't take my lunch to the park. Blame the King, I'll tell her, if Mrs. Liang joins me. The King's ambitions brought murder on his head. Maybe she'll come if her condo gets too lonely. The birds in the park don't have much to say. If I go back to Little House, Ronnie and Gloria will make room for me at the table. What will we talk about? What do they know of war?

For Sale
By Owner

A sign has appeared in our front yard, *For Sale By Owner*, white letters on stiff red cardboard, tacked to a wooden pole and hammered into the grass by my father. He has written our telephone number into the blank space on the bottom of the sign, and the whole appearance of it—the wobbly sign, the careful black numbers, the clear plastic sheeting stapled by my mother so autumn rains won't run the ink—has a whiff of shame about it. There's nothing to be ashamed of though. I don't know why I feel embarrassed. We're going to California. My father has got a promotion. Our ticket up and out—that's what my parents say behind closed doors.

I like the place we live in, a small town out the Philadelphia

Main Line. It's the early sixties, something is stirring, but our little neighborhood hasn't been touched. From the road, we look no different from all the other families around us. Our house is red brick with black shutters. The driveway runs straight, with a basketball hoop for my older brother and me. Yew bushes line the path to our front door. We have a red metal flag to raise and lower on our mailbox. I'm ten; my name is Charley. My family is Chinese—there's no way around that—but we've been welcome here all the same.

I have a pack of friends; they're all envious. They want to be going to California. It seems a joke, that we're moving to Los Angeles. To palm trees and Hollywood and Disneyland. They punch me for that, roll me in the dirt. We scrabble for handholds, trip the ones just getting to their feet. When we come up for air, we laugh at Wally Mitchell, who has weeds in his red hair that make him look like a farmer. Farmer Mitchell, we start to call him. It makes him mad, so we link arms and chant that at him all the way down the block. It's his turn today, but tomorrow it will be somebody else's. The gang keeps track; nobody is the victim for long. I belong here, I know it, and my parents are wrong to think that we're better than this.

Once, only once, did something bad happen. It wasn't scary, only unpleasant. It might have been one of my gang who did it, or one of my brother's friends—he's sixteen. We had a little statue that came with the house; he stood at the end of our driveway. A riding jockey, with a red cap and striped pants, lifting a lantern in his curled hand. It was hard to tell if he was a boy or a man. My father didn't like it, said it wasn't meant for an ordinary neighborhood, a cramped little house like ours, but my mother wouldn't let him remove it. I'll give him a coat of paint then, said my father, and he painted the hands, the grinning face, the feet bright white, with a brand-new can of paint he bought at the hardware store. And the very next day, someone painted slanty eyes across the whitened face of our happy jockey.

Okay, said my mother, her own eyes narrowed. Take it to the junkyard. She hurried back into the house.

It was only a joke, my brother and I protested. We found it funny, because our friends thought it so, but our father's silence as he loaded the little statue into the trunk of the Pontiac shut down our explanations. It was our parents who couldn't see the humor. We knew nobody meant us any harm.

In fact, it's their fault. They go out of their way to be different. My mother, especially, makes it a point. She sends my father to the city—sometimes Philadelphia, sometimes New York—to Chinatown to buy ingredients. She cooks for two days—eggrolls, wontons, mein noodles—Peter and I eat as fast as we can sneak it. Then she and my father put up the green card table and the red one and invite everybody in. My father pours the drinks; the neighbors stuff their mouths full. Wives sing my mother's name across the crowded room. Their husbands put their arms around her waist. She flaps her hands, turns their compliments away. It feels like a circus, the noisy house, the people all clapping, and my parents like performers doing their tricks onstage.

A sign has gone up in my classroom, too. My teacher, Mr. Franklin, has covered the big black-rimmed IBM clock with a poster that says "TIME PASSES. WILL YOU?" So we can't see how long till recess or lunch or the end of the day. Mr. Franklin is a Negro. My mother isn't happy about that.

But I can't take my eyes off Mr. Franklin. He's a big man, with broad shoulders and large hands that are very pink on one side. His fingernails are clean and smooth. He wears a gray suit or a brown one, with a skinny tie and a silver tie clip. The tie clip looks like my father's, except it's plain where my father's is marked with a symbol which he told me means that he's an educated man.

Mr. Franklin does things different. He doesn't ask anyone can he change the rules. He lets me read anything I want to read, and he whips any boy who makes a ruckus. I don't spare the rod, he told us right off the bat. What's that, spare the rod, only Eddie Andrews knew, whose mother is a Baptist. On the playground, Eddie told us that we better look out for a beating.

All the other teachers at Pennwood Elementary are women. Mr. Franklin can do what he wants.

The first time one of us gets a whipping, I see it happen from well out of the way. Gregory Smith is goofing off near the windows, and Mr. Franklin grabs him by the shirt collar and hauls him to the boys' bathroom. No warning—he just grabs him and goes. He has Gregory in one hand and a yardstick in the other. They come back ten minutes later. I'm back in my seat by now, and the whole class is quiet. Gregory wipes his eyes and his nose and sits right down. Mr. Franklin leans the yardstick up against the chalkboard; one end is broken off. We find it on the bathroom floor at recess.

Gregory tells his parents, but they don't show up at school, because Gregory's father uses his belt on his children. And the next day, Mr. Franklin hauls somebody else to the bathroom, Buddy Flintock, who's a Negro too. Buddy breaks the other end of the yardstick. So now we all know that Mr. Franklin plays fair.

"I hereby give my permission for Charley Wu to take any book he wants out of the library," says the note I keep in my desk. It's signed by Mr. Franklin. The librarian works her mouth the first time she reads it. She pinches her lips like she's tasting something awful. I open the books to get her to stamp them. John Steinbeck, Samuel Clemens. She says that Mr. Franklin hasn't got any right. It's she who runs the library, not some fifth-grade teacher. "Fifth grade"—I think she means something else. She stamps the books anyway. She's afraid if she doesn't, he'll come through those doors himself.

Why doesn't my mother like Mr. Franklin? It's not me who's getting the beatings. My father doesn't listen to her when she complains. Charley is learning, is all he says. My brother asks, does he play the radio when he's in there during recess? I go back into the classroom one day to check. Yes, I tell my brother, he plays it loud. Hillbilly music. It's just a joke I'm telling. Mr. Franklin was in there grading papers.

Twenty-three five is how much our house costs. The number puzzles me. I don't know where the zeros are supposed to go. I hear my mother telling Mrs. Dalton, our neighbor, Twenty-three five. I think we should have an agent, but Robert insists on doing it himself.

There will be other Chinese people in Los Angeles, says Peter. We're in the woods, searching for box turtles next to the creek. Aunt Betty is there, for one.

Who cares, I say. None of our friends will be there.

Mother cares. Father cares too.

They're stupid, I tell him. They make a big deal out of nothing.

Twenty-two seven, my mother tells my father. Or get the agent; he'll sell it fast enough.

Be patient, says my father. It just went on the market.

Betty has found a ranch house she wants us to come out and see.

My father says, I can do it by myself. We'll need a new car to drive all the way west.

Now I feel bad, hoping nobody wants to buy it. If there were a buyer, my mother would leave my father alone.

He does things for Peter and me. Twice a month, he takes us to the city to do what rich people do. We go hear an orchestra, or see a boring play—no music, just talking—or watch people dance, or listen to the piano.

I wish he'd stop trying to make us better.

I've got tickets for this Saturday, he says. Only three tickets, because they cost a lot of money. Mother seems happy that she doesn't have to go. It's the ballet again, to see some Russians. I can't stay home though my gang is asking.

We hurry from Penn Station to the bus to the street. There's no time for dinner; he lets us get a sandwich from the Automat, which we love, and a huge piece of lemon meringue pie, which jiggles on the plate like a wagging pet. I am tired before the ballet begins. My father leans forward; Peter and I sag back. The people dance on and on and on, mostly girls in stiff skirts waving their arms up and down. Once in a while, a man jumps out and carries a girl around. We're way up in the balcony, and it's hot. I sleep before intermission.

He's up next, says Father, checking his program. He's bought me a Coca-Cola so I can't say that I want to go home.

Rudolf something-Russian. He tells me again, but as soon as he says it, I can't remember the name.

Mr. Rudolf dances, and everybody roars. He jumps a lot. He spins. I sleep near the end; my father has to wake me. It's past midnight when we get home, but my mother has left the lights on so the whole house is blazing. She argues when my father tells her not to waste money. What's a few dollars next to my personal safety? It's the only way I can get to sleep. Mrs. Dalton told me that just two blocks over, a house was robbed and all the lamps broken. People from the city, says my mother with meaning. This neighborhood is changing. We've got to get out.

———

Here is how my mother and Mr. Franklin meet.

I don't want to move, I burst out one day, to Mr. Franklin, in the classroom during recess. He lets me come in for extra math work when I want. My parents say we have to go to California. I like it here, but they won't listen.

You're moving?

I nod.

He looks at me for a while. Maybe he's sorry I'm leaving? Only Wally Mitchell is better than me at math. Then Mr. Franklin takes a big breath and looks back down at his work. Got to go with the folks, he says. He's telling me to be manly. Got to go where the work is. He looks up again. Your dad get a new job?

I nod. I look at his broad chest and settle my shoulders an inch.

What about your house? he asks.

I guess it's for sale, I say.

How much are they asking?

I don't know what it means, but twenty-three five, I say.

He thinks about that for a moment.

How many bedrooms?

Two, and a den. And a kitchen with a window and a living room for parties. And a yard, I say, because now I see a way to do something nice for Mr. Franklin, who's the best teacher I've ever had, and for my father, who has promised my mother that he can sell the house by himself.

Two bedrooms.

And a den. You should come see it.

I might just do that.

You could come this weekend.

He writes down our address, and then he tells me it's his turn to pick somebody to lead the Pledge of Allegiance. He's talking about the all-school assembly. Everybody gathered in the gym, and one kid up on stage all by himself with the flag. I show him how straight I can stand with my hand on my heart. You lead us on Monday then, says Mr. Franklin. I race out the door, looking for Peter. I mean to tell him about Monday, the all-school assembly, and that Mr. Franklin might buy our house, but when I get out of the schoolyard, the gang is waiting, and we decide to ride our bikes to the highway culvert, where we play half-crouched in the dirt and water, daring each other to crawl all the way to the end. I don't remember Mr. Franklin until it's too late.

My mother is giving Mrs. Dalton a cup of tea when Mr. Franklin rings our doorbell.

Charley, see who it is.

It's my teacher! My voice squeaks, I'm so excited. He's in my house! He's just as big—even bigger—than at school. He has his gray suit on. His tie is knotted tightly; his hat is in his hands.

I don't understand, says my mother to Mr. Franklin. Mrs. Dalton is sitting very still. Is Charley having a problem with his schoolwork?

He wants to look at our house! I shout. Maybe he wants to buy it. He needs a house; he's new at school this year.

My mother's eyes dart to Mrs. Dalton's. Something passes through the air.

Charley is a great salesman, says Mr. Franklin. The house sounds pretty good for my family and me. We have a little baby and we're looking for a nice house in a neighborhood close to school.

My mouth hinges open. I think of Mr. Franklin as one person only.

I'm sorry, says my mother. She's smiling at him. She never smiles so big.

The house is not on the market.

I hear Mrs. Dalton's teacup set back in its saucer.

I see, says Mr. Franklin. He lifts his hat like he's pointing it at her.

Father hasn't taken the sign down, I protest. I've just figured out that she means, it's not for sale.

Charley was mistaken, says my mother, still smiling. I'm sorry you bothered to come all this way.

His hat wavers. His eyes are hard. I'm standing in the middle, and I feel a thick muscle, like a serpent, twist between them, like a rope come to life with a jerk at either end.

He leaves quickly after that. And my mother and Mrs. Dalton collapse in their chairs and shriek.

All the next day I worry should I speak. Tell my father what happened or approach Mr. Franklin. It's Sunday, and we go to church, and Mother serves a good Sunday supper, but I am troubled and cannot eat.

Can I have your pie, says Peter. And my father helps clean up, then goes to his den to listen to his records. I listen for a while too, standing outside the door. I listen longer in the hallway than I do in the concert hall. Better not to mention Mr. Franklin's visit. All my father wants—I'm beginning to understand—all Father wants is a glimpse of beauty.

And on Monday morning, I don't find time to speak to Mr. Franklin, and anyway, what words would come. It's raining, the bus is late, and I need to get my hair combed down before it's time for assembly. Mr. Franklin leads us into the gym. There is the flag on its pole at the side of the stage. All the other classes crowd in, the first-graders, looking like babies, and the sixth-graders, shoving us hard as they roll to their seats. The student band gathers at the steps to the stage. Principal Melton tests the mike, the older boys mocking him by bobbing their heads like chickens. He nods to Mr. Franklin. I try again to flatten my hair, and just as I start to get up from where I'm sitting, Mr. Franklin calls Wally Mitchell to lead the Pledge.

Farmer Mitchell. His red hair sticking up like a nasty finger shoved in my face. I fix my eyes on Mr. Franklin; he has his hand over his heart and his lips are moving. He checks on the class to make sure we're saying it too. When his gaze hits me, I search his face for a reason. I know the reason but anyway I search. He shows me nothing. I would rather see him angry. When the whole school sits, I stay on my feet, glaring at Mr. Franklin until Mitchell returns to his seat.

The grown-ups, they've given me no choice. I pick a fight on our way back to the classroom. Not with Wally Mitchell—that would be childish, and besides, he's my friend. I am being manly now, like Mr. Franklin wanted. I go after Buddy Flintock, one of the Negro boys, one of three. His friends jump in as soon as I trip Buddy. Hands flail, feet are kicking. Head aimed low, I picture myself with horns. Then I feel the grip on my button-down collar, know Mr. Franklin is dragging me away.

The boys' bathroom smells of cold cement and cigarettes. No one is in there but Mr. Franklin and me. Drop your trousers, he commands: the order shocks me. None of the boys beaten before me have admitted to the rest of us that the whip was laid across their flesh. I hear the whistle of the rod as it travels to my body. One, two, three strokes upon me. After the first, I give up and cry. The stick doesn't break, which is all the more shaming, because I know that Mr. Franklin isn't beating me very hard.

My mother finds the welts though I try to hide them. She's come into my room without knocking; never mind that on my last birthday I hung a sign to keep her out. Her loud cries bring my father rushing. They all examine me: Mother, Father, Peter, crowding in. I see my mother trembling in her rage. She demands an explanation. I have a choice to make between my mother and Mr. Franklin, with Father waiting to hear what I have to say.

I could have blamed it on the black boys, as my mother expected. Or the Negro teacher who made us lower our pants to give us those beatings he liked a little too well. I could have sent up the cry and alarm throughout the neighborhood, and with the right story, Mr. Franklin would have been gone.

I chose the other: to tell what Mother had done. I knew she had acted wrongly, and Father, I was certain, would know it too. Maybe I thought, mistakenly, that Father would help me out of my shame and confusion, or thought I would repay her for treating me still like a child. What I remember now is that I told the story simply, and that my mother suffered conscience enough to listen.

But Father failed me, as fathers eventually must. He turned his back on me and spoke only to Mother. A stream of Chinese, much too fast for Peter and me. What little I caught was all about money. The house and the agent and the price that had to drop. Not a word in there about Mr. Franklin or Charley. He ended by throwing his arm down by his side, the most violent thing I've ever seen from my father, and stalking outside to yank the sign up out of the grass. Within a day, another sign; no price named, just the agent. Within a week, the house sold and the movers hired. My father never praised me for knowing right from wrong. Silence was his currency, the value of one's actions never acknowledged or declared. How many years of silences yet to come! When I said good-bye to Mr. Franklin, I couldn't get the words "I'm sorry" out of my tender mouth.

But in the silence, always an intimation. And there is this, that I remember. We are living in Los Angeles some months later. The streets of Watts are burning; the blacks have risen to speak with fire this time. My mother is fearful, fairly crouched in her bedroom, all the lights turned off because now she feels safer unidentified, in the dark. We are miles away, but the fires are spreading. Peter has been told not to drive anywhere but straight home. Once in a while a siren passes, and my mother cowers, hand over her heart. I see my father standing in the front doorway. Close the door, my mother is pleading. He turns on the porchlight to signal his attention. He seems to be listening to a distant din. And his face glows in the yellow light, with a rapture I saw take him the night Nureyev danced.

Prank

The press had the names in time for the evening news. Chan, leaving the hospital with one hand lightly bandaged and his tanned face untouched, checked his cell phone and saw he had fifteen calls. The ER nurse had told him that reporters were calling. You're a hero, she had said, saving that girl like you did. The phone rang again, and he grabbed it.

"Is this Kang Yan Chan?" The woman said his name like a rhyming ditty.

"Chan," he told her. When he let them say "K.Y.," the joke "Jelly" usually came next. "Who's calling?"

"The *Daily News*. What can you tell me about the students who did it?"

Chan readjusted the ear bud for better reception. "It was senior prank day," he explained. "I don't know who did it. Maybe a whole group of them. I saw a girl on fire and I rolled her in the dirt before I knew what I was doing." Normally, he liked to plan things out on the quarter system. He hadn't known that he could act like that, on instinct.

"They were all high school seniors. That's what I've been told." Chan heard the sound of pages flipping and then the reporter yelling across the room, "I'm talking to the guy. Right now. I'm talking to him." She came back on, and Chan checked his collar and smoothed his hair, another instinct, more natural to him than heroics. "A boy named Jamie Phipp," said the reporter. "Brad Millgrove, he was there too. And a third kid, the ringleader. A boy named Anthony Gao."

Chan sat down abruptly on a low cement wall, vaguely aware of the dust and the seat of his trousers. He turned his back to a couple of people walking by. Phipp he knew well—Principal Shunt had suspended him last year when he persuaded two freshmen to hang a dead skunk by its paws in the band shack. And Millgrove was too thick to say no to Jamie. But Anthony Gao he knew only by reputation. A model pupil and a violinist with an unblemished record and a four-year scholarship to Steuben College in the fall. Not the kind of student who spent time in Chan's office.

"Are you sure it was those three?"

"They've already come forward. How about Anthony, what do you know of him?"

"May I ask you to call Principal Shunt?" said Chan. Shunt would yell down the roof if Chan messed up with a reporter. Jesus H., he would shout. This looks bad for me down at the district.

"Just give me some background then. You must know something of this boy, since you're of like disposition."

"Come again?" said Chan. Didn't she have any questions about what Chan had accomplished? He was still amazed that he had raced across the quad and tipped Cherry Edgarton over. He had rolled her all the way to the bushes like the bundle of sod he had laid on his lawn last weekend. She wasn't all ablaze, the way you see those monks in the pictures, who have set themselves on fire to protest one thing or another; it was just her jacket that had sprouted a tongue of orange, but still it was incredible how quickly Chan had reacted and then how gently he had lowered her while she was screaming. Wasn't the reporter going to ask him about that? "I hope you're not suggesting that I would set off a bomb in the middle of the schoolyard."

"Like condition, if you will. Like situation," said the reporter.

Chan, still waiting, made a noise in his lean brown throat.

"Like race," said the reporter, exasperated.

"Oh right," said Chan, and he started to laugh, the presumption being so ludicrous. As if Chan the Californian might have some special insight into Anthony Gao, the Chinese immigrant, who had just blown a classmate, and his future, sky high.

———————

"He wasn't the ringleader," said Principal Shunt. He had summoned Chan to his office and told him to shut the door. It was two days later; the reporters had stopped calling. Principal Shunt had done all the talking and sent them away when he was fed up with their questions. It was a prank, he'd insisted. Nobody was seriously hurt, not even the girl who got a little shaken up. No, nobody could be called a hero because the whole thing was not that big of a deal. The police had come and gone, leaving parts of the quad sectioned off with yellow tape. Insurance had picked up Cherry Edgarton's medical bills, and Mrs. Millgrove had bought her a new jacket, a pink one, Chan had heard, with a fur-trimmed collar even though it was spring and this was the suburbs.

"Anthony Gao?" said Shunt. "He's the best we've had in years. Phipp and Millgrove must have tricked him into it. Or maybe it wasn't him. Maybe they're lying." Shunt pointed Chan into the chair the students usually sat in. It had spindly wooden legs and a scratched seat that narrowed from front to back, but Chan was slender and didn't mind the proportions. Shunt's chair was big and wide, like him. He used his gut the way a general uses his medals to make those under him snap to attention. Chan settled comfortably into the rickety chair. He saw Shunt frown when Chan casually crossed his legs, so Chan let his loafered foot drift close to the big oak desk and grinned to himself at Shunt's predictable reaction: a swipe, open-handed, across the gray wisps plastered to his head with palm sweat. Chan was thirty-two, Shunt almost sixty, and from time to time Chan enjoyed reminding Shunt in small but safe ways that Chan had the best years of his career still ahead while Shunt faced the looming exit. In fact, Chan figured that he had a good shot at getting Shunt's job in two years. Only 4 percent of the district was Asian, but Chan didn't think they would hold that against him. Thanks to Gao, Phipp, and Millgrove, Shunt might retire a little sooner. When he got to be principal, Chan would put two chairs in front of the desk, one for him and one for his guest. High school culture made a lot of sense to Chan: it was better to be part of the crowd than to stand out from it. He had done well so far making friends with most of the students.

"Half the senior class was on the student plaza," said Chan. "Six eyewitnesses saw Anthony Gao running away."

"Okay, so he misjudged the situation. He didn't realize what they were doing."

"Are you sure?" asked Chan. He had looked at the boy's transcript. Anthony had gotten the highest grade in AP Chem last year. It seemed pretty clear to Chan that Anthony had done his homework. The three boys had carried sixty-five pounds of sugar and fertilizer in nine brown paper bags onto campus before sunrise and packed them into a concrete garbage receptacle on the edge of the student plaza. It was Anthony Gao, Phipp and Millgrove claimed, who had lit the fuse trailing from an empty can of Mountain Dew and tossed it into the garbage. The bomb spewed flames for thirty feet, caught Cherry Edgarton's jacket and three trees on fire, burned backpacks and bushes, and took out one wall of lockers. It wasn't supposed to, said Phipp and Millgrove. It was meant to draw laughs, the biggest senior smoke bomb in the history of the school. Anthony Gao wasn't talking.

"Steuben College has withdrawn his acceptance, but I'll be goddamned if they had all the facts on this thing. I want you to call them as soon as we're finished and keep on calling as many times as you have to. Sweet-talk them, Chan; that's what you're good at. Explain the situation. Get Anthony back in." Shunt leaned way back; his chair squealed in protest. He was a far-sighted man who glared better obtuse than acute.

"They're not going to take him back. The DA is pressing charges."

"It wasn't his fault! Phipp made him do it."

"Phipp isn't smart enough to screw in a lightbulb."

"Do you know this kid Anthony? Have you ever met him?"

Chan shook his head. Guidance counselor was the title on Chan's door, but he rarely got the chance to shape a lively mind or gently steer a promising student, as he had once pictured himself doing. A helping profession, that's what he had chosen, and budget cuts, lousy teachers, overcrowding, district malaise had slit open the seams of his good intentions as efficiently as a short-handled knife. The good students, like Anthony Gao, didn't need Chan's help and never asked him for it.

"Call the family in," said Shunt. "I refuse to believe that Anthony was behind this." Chan left the office quickly when Shunt pointed to the door.

There was Anthony, lurking at graduation. He had gotten his diploma but he wasn't allowed to walk. Chan saw right away what Principal Shunt had figured: it was hard to believe that Anthony was the culprit. He was a gangly boy, slumped and spotted. He had black glasses that slid to the end of his nose. One shoulder sat higher from carrying so many books, and there was a black spot on the knob of his left collarbone that looked not like a bruise but a permanent scurf on the skin. From the countless hours of practicing the violin, Chan guessed, as he walked past Anthony into the stadium to sit on the makeshift stage. Maybe Shunt was right, and Phipp had made Anthony do it. Maybe Anthony wasn't talking because he was afraid of Phipp. Chan sat down and watched Anthony climb into the stands to watch. He climbed awkwardly, his violin case in hand, almost falling on top of a grandmother who was sitting a row below him. Phipp was a beast, Millgrove even bigger. Anthony didn't look like he could handle either one, so how was he going to get Anthony to lay the blame on Phipp? Chan felt his mouth tighten just thinking about the prospect. He would have to encourage Anthony, comfort the boy, urge him to come forward. He didn't want to do it, and that was an odd feeling: there weren't many assignments that Chan wasn't willing, even eager, to undertake if it helped the school and burnished his own reputation, but there it was, a subtle resistance; he could feel it in the muscles of his face like someone was showing him a picture he didn't want to look at. He looked again in Anthony's direction and saw Anthony raise a hand to wave at a classmate, then drop the hand quickly, afraid, Chan perceived, that the classmate might choose to ignore him. Meek, that's what this boy was, too scared to stand up for himself and, in the process, making everyone else look bad. His pride burned, remembering that reporter. "Like disposition," that's what she had said. Types like Anthony reflected badly on the rest of us, thought Chan darkly, though he knew he needn't worry: his clothes, his hair, his accentless English distinguished Chan from fresh arrivals. Chan looked around at the student orchestra taking their seats on the stage. There were other Asian kids at school who had managed, unlike Anthony, to find their place. It was Chan's job to help them all fit in, to smooth over difference in deference to order. Chan deliberated. Meek was better than belligerent, he decided. At least he knew how to talk to such a student. He would sit the boy down for a heart-to-heart conversation, and then Anthony would do as Chan said.

The orchestra started to play. Chan saw that the first violin chair was empty. The music teacher, Mr. Kenney, must be mad that he couldn't have Anthony, and the empty chair was his quiet protest. The other violinists looked nervous as they played. Chan wondered how much better they would sound with Anthony in that chair. He couldn't help himself: he looked into the stands again, and there was Anthony, starting to wave as before. No, that wasn't right. He wasn't waving. Chan leaned forward to look at him, startled. Anthony was conducting from where he sat, and all the violinists turned to look at him; even Mr. Kenney, standing in front, did a half turn and gave a half smile. Stop that! Chan wanted to shout, or at least to gesture angrily for Anthony to cut it out, when suddenly Anthony stopped and settled his arms at his sides. A second later, Anthony had his violin out. To Chan's amazement, he began to play.

Chan didn't know what to make of Anthony's behavior. The boy was already in trouble, why would he look for more? He decided to wait for Shunt's reaction, but Shunt didn't complain; he hadn't even noticed. All he wanted to know was, had Chan fixed things with Steuben College? Chan called the parents to arrange for a family meeting.

"You want Anthony come too?" the father asked on the phone. He sounded like Chan's father, uncertain of the rules. "Please," said Chan in the friendliest voice he could muster. "This concerns him, so it would be best to have him here. I suggest he write a letter to Steuben College. To the Dean of Admissions, with an explanation. Have him bring me a draft, and I'll look it over." If Anthony got smart and apologized profusely, Chan had a shot at getting him readmitted.

Summer school began. Ten days had passed since senior prank day, and the campus was cleaned up and quiet. Chan walked down to the vending machines for a Coke. Shunt was there, drinking a can of Mountain Dew. Chan had to step back and admire Shunt for that. That's why the man was a survivor. You couldn't show the students that you were afraid or embarrassed. You couldn't show need: that would sink you.

"You talked to Anthony yet?" Shunt asked.

"They're due in a few minutes."

"What's taking so long to straighten things out? You've had days to make this right."

Chan protested; the end of the year had been busy. "Let me do this my way, with diplomacy. Persuasion. That's why you came to me to fix it."

"You think so?" said Shunt before pushing past him. Chan checked his watch and hurried back to his office. He wanted to be seated when the Gaos came through his door.

To Chan's dismay, only the parents showed up.

"Where's Anthony?" asked Chan. The mother didn't answer; she came in and sat. In rapid Chinese, she told her husband to keep quiet. Chan pretended he didn't understand them. He was glad he had the desk between them, that he hadn't followed his silly notion that he and his guests should sit together and chat. He relaxed after looking the parents over. The office was small, but she didn't crowd it, nor did her husband standing right beside. They were little people. Her knees looked brittle; so did his wristbones. They had cheap haircuts and smelled of cooking oil. Chan knew who they were and all their aspirations. He could tell them precisely what they wanted for their son. He spoke to them in English but he slowed his cadence; if they were like his parents, they needed him to do that, and it made him feel generous to do it before they asked.

"I would prefer to meet with Anthony first, alone," said Chan.

"We go first," said the mother. "Then Anthony join us." The father shifted but kept his mouth shut tight. Chan didn't answer. He was sure that he could take control of the situation, but he noticed that the mother didn't look so little anymore. Her feet were planted like the feet of the powerful in ancestor portraits, and her eyes were like theirs, straight ahead and unflinching. She flicked her gaze at him. "Get him back in," she said directly. "He work very hard, get in to Steuben College. And the money, he need that. The scholarship, I mean."

"Hang on," said Chan. "I need to talk to Anthony first. I can't fix anything without his participation."

"You don't support my son!" the mother cried out.

"Mrs. Gao," said Chan, heat rising to his hairline. He sat up straight and tried to explain himself clearly. "This was more than a harmless prank. It was a reckless act with very serious consequences. We're going to have to have an explanation from Anthony. As far as I know, he hasn't accepted responsibility or shown a shred of remorse."

"Nobody died," said the mother. She pulled a newspaper clipping from her pocketbook. "*Near*-Tragedy," she read with disdain.

Chan, startled, mentioned Cherry Edgarton's jacket and the property damage to the school: the lockers alone would cost nine thousand. "The least he can do is write to say he's sorry."

"The lawyer, he say no," said the father. "They don't want him put anything down on paper." He swayed as he spoke, unable to lift his eyes any higher than the sprightly pony on Chan's willow green shirt.

"But what did he tell you?" asked Chan. "Whose idea was it? Anthony's or Jamie's?"

Mrs. Gao nodded sagely, in agreement with all that Chan had said. "You are right," she told him. "The American boys made him do it."

"I didn't say that! I said I want Anthony to be the one to tell me."

"Maybe we talk to the principal," said the mother. "He understand the situation."

"He put me in charge," said Chan hotly. He was trying to stare her down, but she was looking around his office. Her eyes fixed on a photograph of Caren, Chan's girlfriend, who smiled from a silver frame on his shelf. He saw her study Caren's blonde brightness, and a consoling lash of pride trembled his veins briefly. They weren't dating anymore—he should put away the picture—but that didn't diminish her sunny beauty. He smiled at Mrs. Gao and crossed his hands on his desk. Mrs. Gao smiled back—bone-disintegrating sight! Chan practically crossed his eyes trying to find someplace else to look.

"Okay," she said to Chan. "We go and get Anthony."

"Right now?" said Chan. He had thought he was ready but now he wasn't sure.

"This Chinese," said the mother in disgust to her husband, her Chinese firing like pistol shots through the office. "He thinks he's better; that's why he doesn't want to help."

Chan swallowed, angry at her insult. He saw her stare again at Caren's picture, and this time he didn't want the mother looking. He remembered their break-up, how Caren had stung him, calling him inscrutable after they argued one night. Don't you say that! he had shouted. You might as well call me a Chink, an Oriental! "I said *impervious*," she had cried, flinging her hair and stalking out.

He should reach up right now and knock the picture off the shelf. He imagined the shattered glass bouncing to meet their ankles. It would shut the mother up, fast, if he had the nerve to do it. But he had a better way to fight back.

"You misjudge me," Chan said to her in his rusty Chinese. He didn't let his chin drop when he struggled out the words. He waited for her shock, then her dismay to flicker, but the mother only smiled: Chan had risen like a flounder to her bait. Chan sat there, furious, unable to gather his wits. The mother hummed, looking out the window.

The father went to fetch Anthony from the car, happy to scramble away. By the time he returned, Chan had pulled himself together. He ordered the parents to wait outside and that, at least, felt like retribution. Anthony stood there, shifting from foot to foot. He was clutching his violin case and wearing an old man's type of jacket—gray, thin cotton, with a zipper brass-bright. No self-respecting teenager would be seen in such a garment. Now that he was back in charge, Chan felt more irritated than angry. The boy's meekness rankled him worse than a hateful mouth. Didn't Anthony know the first rule of immigration? The parents were foreigners, but their children belonged. Let the parents be the ones to arrive hat in hand. To force open the iron slab and wedge a stubborn foot in the door. It was the children's job to walk through that door as though they were strolling on a private landscape, a beach or a mountaintop they had every right to enjoy. Shufflefoots like Anthony ruined the view for everyone.

"We meet at last," he said to Anthony. It sounded melodramatic so he tried coming around the desk. He gestured for Anthony to sit while Chan leaned casually against the front of his desk. Anthony, like his father, didn't meet Chan's eyes but put his violin on the floor and carefully watched it.

"What I meant to say," said Chan, reaching back for a pen to twist between his fingers, "is that we haven't yet had the pleasure of meeting. Now that we have, I'd like to help you."

Anthony looked up. "No thanks," he said in a friendly manner.

"It's a delicate situation, but I can make a few calls. I mentioned to your father that a letter from you would help. Can I see your draft? Did you bring it with you?"

"I sent the letter already. It wasn't too hard to write."

"I see. You sent it." Chan couldn't decide whether to move or stay put. He compromised by shifting his weight to the balls of his feet, but he didn't change his face, not even to wipe his smile. "And in this letter, you offered an explanation?"

Anthony paused. Chan waited for his shrug. He had seen this behavior in other students, the nonchalant insouciance that covered a quaking heart. But Anthony didn't shrug. He thoughtfully nodded. "I said what I wanted to say," he told Chan.

"Was it Phipp?" Chan demanded, deciding to cut to the chase. Sometimes provocation got a student talking. Lots of students had tried provoking Chan before, though of course he was wise to them. "Did Jamie get you to help or maybe trick you into it? Did Jamie and Brad bully you into this mess?"

Anthony laughed. He had clear brown eyes, full of recognition. His voice was strong. He sounded Californian. "Is that what they told you? That I got beaten up?"

"I can help you explain, if that's what happened. You don't have to be embarrassed. Everybody knows that Jamie and Brad are trouble. You can tell me the truth. I'll keep it between us if you want."

"No thanks. They're my friends. We get along okay."

"Look," said Chan. He walked back behind his desk and sat down so fast the chair almost rolled away. "You need help. I'm here to help you. Cut the games. I've got a job to do. Those so-called friends of yours don't care what happens to you. If we do this together, you could get back in to college."

Anthony stiffened. "I don't need help from you." Ah ha, thought Chan. A student on the defensive. Here, at last, was something he could work with.

"Your mother wants my help. So does your father." Mentioning the parents would surely humble the son. And he had the mother's support, of that Chan was certain. No matter how proud she was, she had made her calculation and knew that Chan's help was the best bet for her son.

"It doesn't really matter to me whether I go to Steuben or not," said Anthony. "Either way, I get to play music. I've got a good teacher here who has a lot more to teach me. I don't have to go away to do what I want to do."

"Mr. Kenney?" asked Chan. "He's not much of a teacher."

Anthony smiled. He looked at Chan with what might have been pity. Chan felt chastened: he couldn't bluff Anthony on matters of music, and the way Anthony was smiling, Chan could tell that Anthony knew he had the upper hand. Chan tried a different tack, one that had often worked before.

"You want to leave home, don't you? You're not going to stay with your mom and dad forever."

"Why not?" said Anthony. Then he laughed at Chan's expression. "I guess you got away," he observed. A statement of fact, not admiration.

"They want you to go. They know you're better off without

them." His own parents had wailed when he left, but they gave him the money and practically pushed him onto the plane.

Now Anthony shrugged. "Don't worry about my parents," he said. "They'll get over it, me not leaving home." He laughed at the irony. Chan was unnerved: most high school kids couldn't do that with such grace. Hypocrisy they spotted a mile away, and injustice they could smell if it was covered in clover, but an irony, especially if it involved their own parents, was usually too full of truth to look at long enough to see it. I'm the same way, Chan suddenly thought. I don't want to deal with this boy who is forcing my face to the mirror.

"The money," he croaked, trying to make Anthony listen. "It will kill your parents if you turn that scholarship down."

"I'll manage," said Anthony. His confidence was outrageous. "I've already got a job and living at home costs nothing.

"Are you saying you don't want to go? Everyone expects me to get you back in."

"Either way, I know what I'm doing." Anthony stood and picked up his violin.

"Don't walk out of here!" Chan said, but Anthony left the office. Chan crept to the door to watch him walk away.

The rest of the week, Chan hung around in the basement hallway, hands in his pockets and sometimes a baseball cap yanked low over his forehead. The practice rooms were there, next to Mr. Kenney's office. Chan was trying to figure out which room Anthony used. He had seen him head down here the day he ambled out of Chan's office. Each time the hallway emptied, Chan went from room to room, nervously pushing his ear to the door until one afternoon, in the very last room at the end of the hall, he heard violin music playing. He thought it was violin. Maybe it was viola? The piece was complicated, full of swoops and swirls, and fast too, with a nervy insistence. Nervy, thought Chan. The nerve of that kid. He thinks he knows better than me how to deal with superiors, how to navigate the system. It was true that the DA had let all three boys plead to a minor infraction, but not because they weren't guilty. Shunt was bragging that he'd pulled the right strings; he had a second cousin in the DA's office. I get things done, Shunt had boasted and elbowed Chan in front of the other teachers. Chan held his breath and listened some more to the music. The notes went so high that it had to be violin. Chan was a jazz enthusiast himself. He put it on whenever anyone came over.

The music stopped abruptly, and the door opened before Chan could get away. Anthony was pale; did he ever go out in the sun? "You didn't call the college, did you?" he said.

Chan shook his head no. He had wanted to but he didn't, not knowing what he should say.

"Good," said Anthony. "I don't want you to. Like I said, I can handle it myself."

"What about your mother?" said Chan and instantly felt foolish that he had betrayed his fear of the fierce Mrs. Gao with her battered pocketbook and bedrock position. But Anthony didn't sneer.

"If they let me back in, I'll tell my mother you did it."

"I'm not asking you to do that," Chan started to protest, but Anthony shut the door and started practicing again.

"Whaddup?" a voice spoke behind him. Chan whirled around, embarrassed to be found with a door shut in his face. It was Mr. Kenney, the music teacher, tonguing the end of his mustache and looking casually through a stack of loose sheet music he held in his hand. He gave Chan a sardonic wink so that Chan understood that the greeting was offered as a piquant reminder that neither adult could talk a teen's language. The wink made Chan feel a little better. Even Mr. Kenney, a popular guy around school, took the measure of the chasm between students and teachers and didn't expect to ever bridge it. This kid hasn't stumped me, thought Chan, reassured. I still know more than he does.

Mr. Kenney jerked his bushy head toward the closed door. "You get him back in to Steuben yet?"

Chan was careful not to say yes or no. "You know him pretty well, I guess. What do you think? Was Anthony the ringleader? Or was it Jamie Phipp's idea?"

Mr. Kenney shrugged. Chan tried to recall his first name but couldn't. Ron? Roger? He'd been at the school forever, twenty-five years, maybe more. He usually ate lunch with the art and film department. They took their sandwiches to the art room and never invited Chan.

"I don't know," said Mr. Kenney. "It could have been Anthony. He doesn't get pushed around, despite his skinny size. Maybe he just wanted to show off a little. What's he told you?"

"Nothing," said Chan. "No explanation. I want to help him but he's refused. I don't know why he won't let me." The wink had made him too quick to confess.

Mr. Kenney looked at him intently. "They're just kids," he said quietly. He put his hand on Chan's forearm. "You can't make them like us more than they want to. You start thinking you need their approval, they get to owning you, and that can be fatal."

"He's such a misfit," said Chan. "I thought I could do him a favor."

"He's tougher than he looks. He knows what he wants, which is better than most, I suppose. What about you?" All trace of the wink had vanished.

"Shunt's mad," said Chan. "He wants to know why I haven't got him readmitted."

"Yes, well. Shunt's an idiot." Mr. Kenney laughed. "He asked you, you know, because he thought you'd be more persuasive."

"I'm glad he noticed," said Chan sarcastically. "I took him through a minefield last year when that tree fell on Jason Stuckey." At least Mr. Kenney thought Chan had talents. He didn't care that Anthony didn't trust him.

"Sorry," said Mr. Kenney, "but I don't think Shunt had your superior negotiation skills in mind. He thinks you're better positioned to make the ask."

"What's that supposed to mean?"

"Minnesota school, hard up for Asians. They tend to congregate on either coast, you know. Shunt thought you could beat that drum a little harder."

"It's outrageous," said Chan, his color rising.

"Don't take it so personally." The wink was back, one eye crinkled. "You're a good politician. Scratch Shunt's back and he'll scratch yours."

"I don't even like the boy," said Chan, unwisely.

"The ones we don't like are the ones who undo us. They know us better than we know ourselves."

Chan scowled fiercely. He didn't like his depths to be plumbed.

He decided to go to the concert in the park. The Youth Symphony was playing, and local restaurants were setting up stalls. Chan told himself it would be a festive occasion. He didn't dwell on the fact that Anthony might be there.

He arrived with dinner and a blanket. He started to sit on the hill in the back and then he saw Anthony climbing the steps to the stage, so Chan headed for a spot near the front of the crowd. He thought of how he had run to Cherry Edgarton's rescue; that was what this felt like, in slow, confounding motion. He realized that all week in his mind he had been writing a letter. *To the Dean of Admissions, Steuben College. Please forgive this otherwise sensible boy.* He would write about the music, Anthony's passion. One small mistake shouldn't stamp out his chance in the world.

The program began, a concerto grosso, string notes sweet in the evening air. Chan tried to follow the melody, distracted by the thought of his letter. He watched Anthony, who was sitting at the edge of a large section of players, leaning forward in his chair, his body not limp or meek at all but surprisingly graceful as the bow arm leaped. He wore a dark suit, same as all the others. Chan was pleased to see how evenly Anthony played, synchronized beautifully with all the musicians around him. The tip of his bow moved in unison with the field of bows surrounding. A breeze gusted; the music got faster, and Chan lost his focus in the notes. He felt a fraud to be sitting way up front. He looked at the people whose space he had invaded. Their faces were still, their bodies relaxed and open. They seemed to know when to breathe and when to rustle. Chan was the one who didn't belong with the music, but Anthony Gao, his bow with a life to behold, claimed with every note his right to be there.

The music ended. Chan, still anxious, joined the happy applause. He pictured himself walking up to Anthony and telling him sincerely how well he had performed. Maybe praise would get Anthony talking, and Chan could finally ask him for an explanation. Of what, exactly, he wasn't certain.

The musicians stood as one and bowed together. Chan saw Anthony look straight down from the stage at Chan. Chan almost waved to him, then lowered his hand to his pocket. Anthony half-smiled and tipped his head in appreciation. Chan felt sure he would say yes to the letter. Should he fax it, he wondered, or send it by e-mail?

Then Anthony did a curious thing. He raised his hand in the air. Five fingers spread wide, like a symbol of some purpose. All eyes in the audience and in the orchestra fastened on Anthony for a heartbeat, maybe two, but Anthony didn't take his eyes off Chan. His hand stretched, then slowly descended. The conductor hadn't noticed; he was still making his bow.

The raised-up hand bothered Chan the rest of the evening. He saw it, starlike, holding its place in the air. Around midnight, it occurred to him that he would never send that letter.

At the end of the summer, Steuben College let Anthony back in. True to his word, Anthony gave Chan all the credit. Chan protested; it was Anthony who had written. Shunt interfered and blocked Chan's name from the district. As far as he was concerned, it was Shunt, not Chan or Anthony, who got things done right.

No note came from the mother. The father, though, brought Chan a big net bag of oranges. He bent his head when he presented them, then backed out of Chan's office, refusing all thanks.

"You write good letter!" he praised as he retreated. "You get my son back in. And the money too!"

Anthony came in once, to deliver a whiplike tail of little red firecrackers, touched in gold.

"I got them off of Phipp," he told Chan with a grin. "He bought them in Chinatown out of some guy's trunk."

"Get those out of here," said Chan crossly. "Someone from the district might walk right in."

He kept Anthony's present in the bottom drawer of his desk until Christmas vacation, when the school was deserted; then he carried the firecrackers out to the football field. The grass underfoot was dry and flattened, and faint white lines still marked the boundaries. He thought he heard music from a radio far away, but when he stopped to listen, he couldn't detect it. He walked to the middle of the stadium, expecting to feel grand, but things looked a lot smaller in the thin winter light. In his pocket was a box of matches. The bleachers were empty, waiting for the explosion. The string dangled crazily, its fuse cut short and quick. Chan lifted a hand to reach for the matches, but all he could manage was a tiny wave.

What
I Know
Now

I was eighteen, a year younger than my sopho-
more classmates, and had come to the university, an illustrious
one with sandstone buildings, red tile roofs, and a chip on its
shoulder, as a transfer student from the University of Nevada.
My parents had used to live in Reno back when it was nothing—
foothills, a neighbor's wave—and I had had use of a horse there
when I was ten, which I rode out to see every day on my bicycle,
so I had gone back to Reno at the start of my freshman year, looking for home, though of course it was long gone.

At my new university, they gave me a plastic ID stamped
Transfer Status, which meant I was guaranteed a place to live
on campus. The university had gotten so flush, despite its sore-

footed self-image, that lots of its students were evicted by their sophomore year and made to leave their hobbit holes, leave their warmed seats at the cafeteria table, and find themselves an apartment near the town railroad tracks, but I was guaranteed housing so that I could integrate smoothly into campus life. I was given three roommates, all sophomores, and assigned to live in 25W, Madera Court, a mobile home parked with sixty other mobile homes, four to a quadrant, and one main office. This trailer park, this temporary housing, arranged along narrow pathways like a child might arrange Band-Aid boxes in repeating patterns across the bathroom floor, had gone in as an emergency stopgap solution, installed for two years, three at the most, in the vacant lot next to an elegant Spanish mission–style dorm known for its spring musical productions. It seemed a joke, a mockery, that the careful sandstone quadrangles of the rest of the university should be imitated in aluminum siding, but no one much noticed the absurd contradiction: my roommates told me that the trailer park had been there going on ten years. Though I had hoped, when I pored through the glossy catalogs and dreamed rich dreams of my collegiate career, that I would be given a corner room in a red-topped tower, it was fitting after all that I should be assigned to the trailers. The year, I recall clearly, was 1974.

My roommates were all Californians, "from the valley," they told me, although they were different valleys. Meghan was from San Fernando; she became my friend. Marquita and Miguela were twins, identical twins, whose parents weren't exactly farmworkers from Modesto but did something that had to do with farming. That's how much I knew. I was young and didn't pay attention, or paid attention to things—phrases, music, glances—things I cannot see or hear and anyway have no use for now. My name being Marsha, it was a great joke to the four of us that we all started with M, a joke made even bigger when four boys moved into 27W, the trailer right behind ours, boys whose names were Matt, Mark, Myles, and Kevin. Poor Kevin, we said. The lone rider. He drew a K on his bare chest with black Magic Marker on warm Friday nights when the beer flowed.

I cannot remember why I took the job tutoring Nikki. I must have felt some odd impulse to do one real-world thing in the unreal world of campus fun, campus pranking. He was five years old and lived with his parents in married student housing. They were worried about him—he didn't know his numbers—and they wanted him to have a little extra help. I suppose what I was thinking of when I heard of this boy and his parents was solid family life, choice made and blessing taken hold of, shared worries and determined settling in, all the things my own life had failed to deliver. My mother was in England by then, my brothers and sister experimenting—at the time of the red Plexiglas bong, at the start of cocaine's regular appearances—with their own renditions of a satisfying home life, and my father spinning between Reno and New York, torn between business and a twenty-two-year-old wisp who had once lived up the street from us and brought me a real grass skirt from Hawaii.

Married student housing. Just walking up the steps and into the building made me feel as though I were crossing over. In the trailers, in the clubs, like play houses where we ate our meals, and in the dormitories I had visited for keggers on Friday nights, every student was a single, even those with boyfriends or girlfriends. Everything was temporary, meant to be experienced for a short, single time, and every coupling was on a trial basis. But here in the high-rise and behind the blank doorways repeating themselves down the long dim hallway were pairs conjoined, their cell walls collapsed and reformed so that ones became two, coexisting. It was a romantic notion, even picturing it as I did, as an illustration in my biology textbook. There was the start of something in those pairs. It gave me a thrill to be walking down the hallway, looking at the numbers on every door and the names pasted under the small, rectangular brass knockers, some names shared, some defiantly different, because this was the era in which women would not hesitate to follow their husbands to graduate school but, if they were adventurous or resentful, kept their own names as a tiny gesture of independence. I took my time walking down the hallway, studying names and apartment numbers, peering when I could into open doors. Were I to make such a walk now, I suppose I would name the pleasure I felt at viewing the evidence of other people's lives prurience—that ugly word and uglier emotion, like the pleasure one gets from ruthlessly tickling a child—but then, as I took my tour of married student housing, I did not know to call the sensation anything other than a thrill.

Stephan opened the door and he looked like a Frenchman's joke. He was shorter than most of the trailer boys I had met, and his shoulders were more narrow, but underneath his red and white striped shirt were a man's muscles, coaxed into prominence by dumbbells and vanity, and his jeans bulged so noticeably at the crotch that I thought he must have an injury there that required padding or protection. His dark head was sleek, against the fashion, and his ears lay flat, another vanity, because I saw a gold earring in the right earlobe, thin gold wire just big enough to draw notice. He had blue eyes in a tanned face. His teeth were bright white. The smile he gave me was probably full of seductive irony—that's how I picture it now—but I knew only that it was not frank or friendly. It made me reluctant to shake his hand.

"And this is Marcie," he said, beckoning his young wife, and we shared a short laugh over the similarity of our names. She was a version of her husband, small and dark, but without his otterlike quality, because she fidgeted, first with her hair, which was too frizzy for her liking, though I instantly envied its chestnut luxe, then with a cigarette, a glass, a magazine. Not once, in my nine weekly visits to married student housing, and the tenth visit, at night, when I thought Stephan would be there, waiting, did I see Marcie's hands at rest by her sides. It made me feel the stupid weight of my own huge hands, a family feature that could be seen in every stiff portrait and photogravure going back five generations, thick, ham-handed hands with sausage fingers and peculiar white nails that looked as though they had been dipped in calcium, hands too big to glove or ring or choose to display as one's distinctive beauty, that hung like buckets at the ends of my twiggy arms.

Then Marcie dragged out Nikki and made him say hello.

"This is Marsha," she told him in her flutelike voice, each word a clear note that charmed me. "She will be your tutor. She is a wonderful children's teacher." She dipped to the boy, but still he hung back, until Stephan spoke to him sharply in French, too quickly for me to understand him. Nikki came toward me one step, so I knelt in front of him and smiled and told him I was looking forward to helping him with his numbers and that I was going to try hard to make it a lot of fun. He held himself stiffly and did not return my smile. He was small and dark like his parents. He looked more like Marcie than Stephan, though I saw Stephan's blue eyes in his little locked face. I knew right away that he wouldn't learn much from me. It didn't matter. I would earn my course credit no matter what progress Nikki made—three units, maybe four, I've forgotten that kind of detail now, from a department I had nothing to do with—sociology or psychology or maybe early childhood education. The subject of the course had little to do with the job, and the job, I could tell, would have little to do with the child. The thrill I had felt at walking down the hallway, looking into the open doors of couples' apartments, still pricked along my forearms and nicked at the back of my neck. I looked up at Marcie; she was looking at Stephan, and he was watching me kneel before his son.

It was an easy term. I had planned it that way, not knowing how I would handle the transfer to California, the all-new friends, and the culture of riches. I had biology, which I enjoyed, and French composition. I had a class in medieval English history that my roommate Meghan and I attended together, sitting way in the back of the uncrowded lecture hall, pretending to be law students, which is what we thought we might someday want to be. I tutored Nikki once a week and kept a journal of his progress, which I had to show now and then to my adviser. There was spare time between the studying and my classes, loads of it. And Meghan and Marquita and Miguela had spare time too, because they were all brilliant and college was easy and none of them had much of a care, graduation being so far away.

We took up two things, the four of us. We volunteered to walk precincts in the gubernatorial election—my first election, the first time I would vote. And we gave regular parties on Friday nights. The boys in 27W would somehow procure a keg and pass the word around to the people we liked in the eating clubs and trailers, and by nine o'clock on Friday nights, the narrow path between 25 and 27W was filled with people laughing and smoking. The music was loud and terrible—Elton John, Peter Frampton—the dope pungent on the warm fall air. There wasn't dancing but there was a lot of singing, lyrics belted out into the night, the boys jumping straight up when a chord came crashing down and the girls admiring their loose, good fun. Around midnight the campus police would sometimes come calling, asking us politely to tone it down, take it inside, and we usually did, calling things to a close with a final number. It was performed by the boys in 27W. It was what they had become famous for, at those Friday-night parties. They took off their shirts and tied them around their heads. They took up air instruments—for Matt, his tennis racket, for Mark, a bottle of beer. Myles used the silver pole that cranked open the screened window in the roof of the trailer. Then they all turned their eyes on Kevin.

What he did never failed to draw a laugh. He had discovered, one afternoon, while lying on the moss green carpet of their trailer and poking with his bare foot at the edge of the college-supplied sofa, that the wood veneer facing of the sofa frame was loose. It came off, after prodding, in one long piece: the whole length of the frame and the dogleg handle of the sofa arm. That was his air instrument, the wood veneer frame, and he took it off every Friday night for use as a bass guitar.

"Secret AG-ent Man, Secret AG-ent Man," the boys shouted, working the air hard to their favorite oldie and pounding their white-sneakered feet. The trailer rocked and shook like it might fall off its footings. The rest of us sang too, but we let the four of them lead us, Kevin whirling and stomping out front, brandishing his piece of the sofa, the sweat slick on his chest. We got them to perform it every Friday night, and then the crowd peeled off, most of the people in pairs that might or might not last the weekend. Miguela and Marquita had boyfriends, seniors, who had apartments and cars of their own, so they usually left with a wave and a car-door slam. The boys in 27W did what they could with whoever had showed up that night. Kevin, always, had a girl to go home with. Meghan and I cleaned up a little. We sometimes made cocoa or had a last beer and fell asleep in our bunk beds, metal ones, like the trailer, because we had been unlucky and had drawn the double room. And in the morning, after the girls who had spent the night in 27W had stumbled back to their dorm rooms and row houses and Meghan and I had finished cleaning up, the boys would finally wake and come to our trailer, where we would have a pot of coffee ready and we would visit until Kevin showed up and the boys went off to the Saturday football game.

I didn't pay much attention to Nikki in those weekly visits, but what they wanted him to learn was too much. He did know his numbers, and he could count by twos all the way to twenty. He knew easy addition and even subtraction from ten, but Stephan wanted him to learn his multiplication tables.

"I knew these numbers when I was Nikki's age," Stephan told me, his teeth showing white in a friendly smile. "And Marcie, she is good with mathematics also. She was studying mathematics before we came here, so Nikki has the genes"—he laughed—"for knowing his numbers too."

I said I would try to teach him. It was false, what I promised, but I wanted the course credit and I didn't think I would do him any harm. I went to him on Wednesdays at five o'clock and stayed for an hour at the kitchen table. I showed him picture books with bright red and blue numbers and recited the times tables in a cheerful voice, hoping that singsong would lure him into learning. Around five thirty, Marcie came into the kitchen to prepare the family supper. And five or ten minutes before I was to leave, Stephan came through the door, carrying his books and the front wheel of his bicycle. He kissed Marcie twice, he kissed Nikki, and he leaned close so I could show him the weekly lesson.

"This is good," he would say, seeing the bright pictures. "Nikki, are you attending?" He would brush his fingers over the page where my hand was resting. I let it rest there, the thick meat of it, covering most of the page, most of the whole book, and he brushed his fingertips right up against me.

"I'm looking for some other teaching aids," I would tell him, "to make it more fun for Nikki." I hadn't a clue how to go about tutoring Nikki. I couldn't recall how I had learned the tables myself. My mother must have taught me while she was making supper, or my father, playing games with me on a Sunday drive. I didn't think I had learned them in the classroom. The good things, the important things, I had learned at home from my two parents.

During one session, I think it was the third or fourth, Nikki rebelled.

"No!" he suddenly protested. He knocked the book I was holding from my hand. "I don't know it, I don't know it!" He tried to get down from the table.

"Nikki," said his mother, coming quickly into the kitchen. I wondered whether she listened to our lessons every week. She took his arm gently and coaxed him back into his chair. "You're not a baby anymore. You can learn this. It is easy."

"No," said Nikki again, but he turned his face to his mother and put his hands, folded, back on top of the table.

"Let me show you something," she said in a stagy whisper. She went to a kitchen cabinet and pulled out a Mason jar. She brought it to the table and had Nikki unscrew the lid. The jar was heavy, full of dried kidney beans, and he struggled with it for a moment, but he got the lid off and showed it proudly to his mother.

"Now we count," said his mother. She poured a stream of beans onto the table; some of them fell to the floor, which didn't bother Marcie. Nikki began counting, by twos, by fives, until he had a pile of thirty beans on the table. Marcie swept a few extras back into the palm of her hand.

"Now," she said with a brief nod of her head at me. I paused, knowing what to do but unsure whether I should continue. She was home, Marcie, with Nikki every day. She knew better than I did how to teach her son his numbers. I looked over at her, and she was looking down, screwing the lid back onto the Mason jar, screwing it tight and tighter still, so that I knew it would not come off the next time without a sharp tap or a splash of scalding water.

"We can do it like this," I said to Nikki. I showed him two beans three times; I showed him three beans twice. I ran him through the two times tables all the way to twenty and back. When Stephan walked in half an hour later, Nikki was reciting "two times six" for me and pushing the beans back and forth on the table.

"Brilliant," said Stephan with a laugh. "You are a natural teacher, Marsha." He glanced at the kitchen; Marcie wasn't there. "And your hair looks very nice today." He almost touched it. "I like it up like that."

I didn't tell him the beans were Marcie's idea. I just had Nikki go through the basics again.

The twins' boyfriends seemed almost twins themselves. They were short, like my roommates, and cheerfully healthy. They were engineering students who worked harder than the rest of us, and their families were rich, which made me feel awkward. The four of them, the twins and their boyfriends, took a daily run from our trailer steps to the satellite dish at the top of the campus, miles away up a dusty trail. They said from up high they could see the trailer park. It stood out, they said, among the red tile rooftops, an eyesore, the ugliest section of campus. They were planning to get a house next year, the four of them said. There were some nice houses on the south side of town, too far for the girls to bike to, but with the two cars between them, the four could make do.

Mid-October came, unseasonably hot. The trailers turned into long metal cookers, with us roasting in our rabbit-hutch rooms. We slid open all the windows, but they were too small to make any difference, so we opened the front door and the back door, hoping to create a breeze. There were no screens on the doors, but the bugs left us alone. The trailer park had been so precisely laid out that when all the doors were open, in every trailer in the park, one could look down a row and see through every dwelling. There was one long view through the front and back doors of 21W, 23W, 25W, 27W, on and down until the edge of the park. But there were no secrets in the trailer park. There was no thrill to peering into those doorways. Every trailer looked the same—paneled walls, moss green carpet, and undersized refrigerators humming like mad. Standard-issue chairs were dragged into the courtyards, and some people even brought their mattresses out at night; it was too hot to sleep or study in their rooms. Our Friday-night parties had grown a little stale. We skipped one week and liked not having to clean up.

Then the twins' boyfriends, Christian and Dennis, brought us our precinct assignments. Meghan and I were to walk three precincts in town, reminding people to get out to vote and hanging flyers on doorknobs. It was, as I say, my first election and it was 1974, when all the country was bruised and battered and Californians wanted badly to stand apart from the nation's mess. It was my first time out but I knew what I wanted. I was working for a man who wanted to be governor, a young man, trained by priests, a man proclaimed different, whose eccentric egotism I mistook for humility and a calling. I was to knock on doors for that man. I was to ask people to get out and vote.

But Meghan was sick the day we were to walk precincts and I didn't want to do it alone. It was still hot, too hot for the end of October, even in the late afternoon after classes. The trailer was broiling. I changed into a skirt and a lemon-colored peasant blouse. I put in orange button earrings, tiny flowers at their center. My sandals were brown and my legs brown too, firmed up after all the bicycling around campus. I walked out our back door to 27W to see who might be around to help me knock on doors.

No one was there but Kevin. He was sitting on the couch, a glass of water in his hand, reading a book required for one of his classes. His hair curled up in back where it hit his collar. He was clean-shaven and smelled of Dial. It occurred to me that I had never seen him so still. And the glass of water moved me, being clear and simple and unexpected in his hand, just as it might move me now, because I have not wholly left behind the girl who stood in that trailer, one leg stuck behind the other. She pains me, that girl, she embarrasses me still, but I hold on to her fiercely in her momentary visitations, the girl with no money, no parents, and no place. The glass in Kevin's hand glinted in the afternoon sun. I hadn't thought to notice before whether the boys owned glassware, the little comforts of a home.

"Will you come walk precincts with me?" I asked. He looked up slowly.

"It's almost dinnertime," he said. "People will be eating."

"That's when you're supposed to do it," I said. "Then you know people will be there."

"I'm supposed to do this," he said, looking at his book. He had left his finger in the page where he'd been reading, but his arm was already straightening, getting ready to drop the book on the floor. I noticed his hair again, still wet from his shower. His feet looked strong, bare against the carpet. The sofa he had put back together again, as he did every week after his performance. You couldn't tell that the frame of it came right off in your hand.

"I'll make you dinner later," I promised. "Though it has to be eggs. Omelettes are all I know."

"Eggs are good," he said, standing. He tucked his shirt into his jeans. When we walked out the front door, he put his hand on my elbow.

I remember one house that Kevin and I visited that day. Or not the house, really, only the front porch. It was painted Cape Cod blue, not a California color. It had a low railing and a hanging eave. Vines grew up and around the porch. You couldn't see the front door from the sidewalk; we didn't even know if the house was lived in. We stood uncertainly on the porch for a moment before we found the bell, a little rusted thing that had a pull string, like something you would find on a farmhouse. Kevin reached across me to pull the string. I leaned into him when he did that, and he turned and kissed me, right before he rang. We held our mouths together and parted slowly. An exact right kiss at the exact right time. We turned back to face the door. Our hands brushed, and he folded his fingers lightly into mine.

A woman came to the door, old and distrustful. I told her why we were there and held up the flyer with the handsome picture on it.

"That phony," she said sharply. She waved us back from the door. "That crank."

I tried again, eager to inform her.

"He lied to his country," she said. She poked at the screen door and held her finger there so that the screen bulged out in one place as though a tall child had his nose pressed against it. "Cheated us all," she said. "Made them tapes and wasn't smart enough to burn them."

Oh no, I told her. That man was gone. The man we were talking about was running for governor. He was young and fresh and he would help California. Had she heard of him? Did she want to know more?

Kevin whispered to me, "Marsha, let's go."

"Get off my porch!" the woman suddenly screeched. She pointed her finger through the screen at Kevin. "I don't know that boy! Get him off my porch!"

"Okay, I'm sorry," I sang out to the woman. I felt Kevin's hand in mine, so I wasn't worried. "Here's something for you to read," I said, but I didn't know where to hang the flyer. There wasn't a knob on her screen door, and I didn't want to open the door and scare her even more. I hung the picture of my candidate on her rusted bell. It stood out to anyone who might follow us up onto her porch. I knew she wouldn't come out to remove it. The mailman would think she was calling for his vote.

It was dark when we took the bus back to campus. Kevin sat close, his one arm loosely around my shoulders, his other across his lap so that he could finger my hand.

"You have amazing hands," he said. He held one up to look at in the bus's harsh light. "Football hands. Giantess hands."

"They do things," I heard myself say. "They go places."

He breathed into my ear.

"Where?" he asked.

"Here," I said, and pushed two fingers against the zipper of his jeans, using his arm as cover. I heard his breathing quicken.

We stumbled off the bus at the first stop on campus, still a long walk from the trailer park, but we wanted the woods, the darkness. We kissed under the trees, under the streetlamps, past the Quadrangle and library and nipple-topped tower. At one corner, he squeezed my breast. At another, I put my whole hand down the back of his jeans and cupped him like a ball.

"Where?" he asked again. I drew my hand out but didn't open my eyes. "Not the trailers," he said. "They'll all be back by now."

"There's no hurry," I said. I kissed him on the mouth again, kissed his throat, pressed my mouth to his sternum.

"God," he said. "Come on," and he pulled me and he hurried me down the path toward the museum. "It's wooded there," he said. "Nobody will see us."

I followed for a few steps, then stopped, confused.

"I don't think I want to do this," I said. "Not out in the open." I felt odd and torn, wanting his mouth again, my hand in his jeans, but knowing also that this wasn't how I imagined it would be, crouching in leaves with clothes still on and my bare ass ground into dirt.

"Marsha," he said. "Come on, come on." He kissed me, I kissed back, but I didn't walk any further.

"Don't do this to me," he said. "You know what it's like. What's wrong? This is great. We could be great together."

"I'm not sure," I heard myself say. I should have stopped right there, but I found myself saying it. "I'm not sure I want Kevin Moore to be the first."

He stopped cold then and made a move of impatience. I felt a full heat flush my face, was glad for the darkness, was already cringing at my confession. It wasn't true anyway; there had been another, a murky thrashing around in the back of a van on the high Sierra road, a boy I had known in Reno who had happened to be driving in my general direction when I struck out for my new life in California. I suppose that's what I was thinking of, or trying not to think of, the boy's urgency and my strange distance, caused, I hoped, by the cold vinyl of the car seat beneath me and the tight tangle of clothing we hadn't removed. I wondered if I could ask for a bed and a blanket and a sunlit room instead of the woods behind the museum, but in those days, it seemed my whole life took place in furtive moments that I felt I should somehow be grateful for. All I could do was stop my mouth against more blunder.

"Yeah," said Kevin briefly. He brushed down my hair, my shoulders, my skirt, like a window dresser straightening the display.

"I'm sorry," I said, but he stopped me.

"Don't apologize," he said with disgust. "Jesus, don't apologize." He held my hand lightly as we walked back to the trailers. He kissed me good night; I knew that would be the last.

——— ———

Election day came. I pushed aside the paper curtain and voted for the first time, holding my breath at the gravity of my act, a life signpost, an arrival. The poll worker handed me a torn stub, proof of my new status—it didn't satisfy; I felt I should be given something more permanent, like a pen or a plaque or at least a metal button. When our candidate triumphed, the twins and their boyfriends took a victory run and returned to the trailer, glowing with their effort. They made themselves fruit freezes and drank them happily, sitting on a beach towel laid out in our cement courtyard, then took themselves off to have a shower. Meghan and I were on our front steps. The days had cooled a bit and it was evening, but it was still warm and stuffy in the trailer. We heard the shower running. We heard Marquita laughing and her boyfriend call for a towel.

"What are they doing in there?" Meghan asked. She listened, her head cocked, while I tried not to. "They're all cramming in," she said. "All four of them, I think."

"I barely fit in there by myself," I said. "There isn't room for all four."

"Well," she said, "they're little." We listened a moment longer. I felt a tug between my legs and wished again for Kevin, as I had been wishing night after night.

"Maybe you're right," said Meghan. "Maybe they're taking turns, two by two. But which two?" She laughed a little. She wasn't happy that I didn't laugh at her joke.

"Christian and Dennis, do you think?" she asked. She nudged me with her elbow. "Or the twins, with the door open, letting the men watch?"

I shoved at her elbow and stood up.

"Don't be a creep," I said.

"Gah-ahd," she replied, unoffended. "The cobwebs down there are getting to you. But look, I'm like you." She waved her hand between her legs. "No action. Nothing going on. I'm getting so desperate, I might have to consider one of the guys next door." She glanced at me and saw my expression.

"You didn't sleep with one of them, did you?" Her eyes darted around the courtyard. Then she stood up next to me to ask again. "Last week? When you were out late with Kevin?"

"No," I insisted. I pressed my thighs together as I said it. "Kevin? Are you kidding? None of them, no." I heard the vehemence in my voice and tried to flatten it out. "They're boys," I said disdainfully. "They're air musicians."

"You had me worried for a second," said Meghan, laughing. "I know we're desperate, but hopefully not *that* bad." She brushed off her jeans. "Let's go for a walk," she said. "I don't want to be sitting here when they come out of the shower."

There was a movie showing all the way across campus. We went to that, and when we got back, the trailer was dark and quiet.

―――――――

My adviser had checked in with Nikki's parents. She praised my work with the little boy, said I was a natural teacher, and she was impressed at how well I had done with an independent project, especially as this was my first term in a really rigorous program. I looked away when she said that, a rigorous program, because I knew I had spent the better part of the fall doing things my scholarship wasn't meant to pay for. What was my final project, my adviser wanted to know. What had I come up with to finish my work with Nikki?

I was making him a teaching aid, bright-colored flash cards in the shape of fruits. I had gone down to the art store, not the small one tucked into the student bookstore but the huge one in town, where I had bought stiff board and razor blades and paints. The fruits I copied from an illustrated children's dictionary, bright red apples for the one times table, golden yellow pears for the two times table. Plums, melons, strawberries, oranges. Ten of each fruit and a fruit for every number, one through ten. The bananas were the hardest: I had cut them too skinny, so it was hard to fit 6×6 on the front and 36 on the back, but I made them all with care and was pleased at the outcome. I knew that Nikki did not like me, did not look forward to my weekly visits, and I had not confessed to my adviser that the creative teaching methods for which I was praised—kidney beans, jump-rope games, tiny marshmallows counted into muffin tins—had all been suggested to me by the boy's mother, but at least I would make Nikki this one, fun thing, and leave it for him and not return. I bought flannel off a long roll at the fabric store. I borrowed a sewing machine from another student. I had the hardware store measure and cut me a dowel, twenty inches long, which fit at the top of the flannel, and I sewed a long panel with pockets for each fruit. When it was done, it looked like something I could sell at the holiday crafts fair setting up in the student plaza. I hung it on the back of our bedroom door in the trailer to give to Nikki at the end of the term. When I saw it hanging there, red and yellow flannel, with colorful fruits,

I remembered that I had had something like it on the back of my bedroom door in Reno, though mine had been for plastic horses, and my brothers had one day pulled it down.

———   ———

Thanksgiving came, and I went home with Meghan. Her parents were kind to me, serving me turkey and cranberry sauce and wine. It was a relief to be out of the trailer, to sleep in a bed in a room by myself without Meghan snoring lightly in the bunk above me. I began looking forward to the next school term. It would be Miguela's and Marquita's turn to take the double bedroom. And in the spring, they said, they would maybe move out and find that house with their senior boyfriends, who had both signed on to graduate studies. Dennis's parents had thought it was a good idea. They had said they might even buy a condo near campus and let the four of them use it while Dennis was still in school.

———   ———

The temperature dropped, then dropped again. I decided to walk to married student housing; I didn't want to take Nikki's present rolled up in my bike bag. I folded it carefully into a shopping bag and tucked tissue paper around the sides. I was planning to surprise him—no lesson at all, just the gift and a good-bye. Or maybe we would try it out together for the hour so that I could say good-bye to Stephan as well.

I entered the building and slowed my steps. None of the doorways down the long hallway was open. I listened for sounds behind the doors; sometimes in the past I had heard laughing and arguments, once even a man crying, but today everyone was quiet. Nikki answered the door when I knocked.

"Where's your mom?" I asked him, surprised.

"She's tired," he said. "She's not coming out today." He pulled me by the hand, the first time he had done that, and I had to slow him down to take off my shoes, which were muddy. The television set in the living room was on, and that surprised me too, because Stephan had rules about television during the day.

"What's this?" I asked. Nikki showed me a tower of blocks hemmed all around by little cars and trucks.

"Are you counting them?" I got down on my knees. I started to count the trucks for Nikki, "One, two, three."

"No!" said Nikki. He clapped his hands over his ears. "Don't count anymore!"

"Nikki," said his father. Stephan had walked in, from the bedroom, I guessed, and was standing over us, smiling. He held out his hand to raise me from the floor. I took it and felt a flush creep over my face.

"We're having a bad day, aren't we Nikki?" said Stephan. Nikki nodded and dashed across the room and back. He waved his arms and jumped a little. The top of the tower toppled; he noticed it and jumped a little more.

"Fall down!" he commanded. "Fall like I told you!" The rest of the tower collapsed, Nikki crowing.

"Shhh," admonished his father. He pointed toward the bedroom and spoke rapidly to the boy. I heard *Maman* and the word for sleeping, but whether he said she was ill or just tired, I couldn't tell with my juvenile French.

"Would you like something?" Stephan asked me. He brought me to the sofa and had me sit down. I said I wanted nothing, but he brought me a glass of wine and sat beside me, our hands almost touching. I couldn't look at him as I drank what he offered. I tried to talk to Nikki, but the boy kept dashing away.

"I can't stay today," I said. "I just came to bring Nikki my final project."

"Nikki," said Stephan. He made the boy come over. "Marsha has a gift for you." He fetched my bag and watched me present it.

"But this is so nice," he said. He smiled at me and touched my hand. "Nikki will love this. Nikki," he reminded.

"Merci," the boy said.

"Show it to Maman," said his father.

Nikki shook his head.

"Show it," said Stephan. He pushed Nikki toward the hallway.

"Maman," said Nikki, dragging the long flannel after him down the hall. Some of the fruits fell out onto the carpet, leaving a trail like Hansel's bread crumbs. I heard the bedroom door open and close. Stephan reached for me. I found myself lowered back onto my knees. Then the blouse open and the hands come round again, and my face gently held, just the way I had always wanted it held, until my head was pushed down and my mouth pressed into service, and my mind fixed itself on a bed in a sunlit room.

Our friends asked us for one more Friday night. Dead week was coming, and then finals. Matt, Mark, and Myles spread the party word. The twins and their boyfriends drove into town for groceries, and Meghan and I cooked a pot of chili.

"One off," said Meghan, licking the wooden spoon. "I've told the men not to get used to this. I don't plan on cooking for them on a regular basis."

It was our best party, that Friday night. Our friends were happy, grateful for the meal and the beer and the music, and the coming hard work didn't spoil anyone's fun. It was a cold, clear night, as cold as a night in Reno, and the stars were out, dozens of them. I looked up and saw them savagely twinkling and saw my breath coming out of my mouth in white puffs, big white puffs I kept huffing out into the night air. From the moon, I imagined, or from a spaceship or a mountain, the trailer park would be gleaming in the dark, an elaborate calculation sketched out across a blackboard, a pattern of lights, one turned to two turned to three turned to four. A few couples had come out with me into the darkness, but most everyone else was inside the two trailers, 25W and 27W, women in our trailer, most of the men in the other, clinking bottles and singing along with the stereo. I heard my friends calling for the final performance. I heard the four roommates of 27W yelling back to the crowd like rock stars.

"You want it?" they yelled.

"Yeah!" cried our friends.

"You want it good?"

"Yeah!"

"You want it now?"

"Yeah!" And the stereo cranked up, and I knew that the four of them—the Ms and Kevin—were jumping and thumping: I could hear the music.

"Secret AG-ent Man—"

"Where's Marsha?" Kevin yelled. I jerked my head up.

"Marsha!" he bawled over the music. The people outside with me starting calling to me to go over.

"Marsha!" called Meghan. She dragged at my arm, pulled me into the trailer. They were all mashed in there, all the singles, all the couples for the night, and Kevin, shirtless, wildly dancing with the broken piece of furniture and a cut on his face.

"Marsha, Marsha!" he cried when he saw me, and he grabbed me and made me swing around. He started doing a bump and a grind and I pushed him away, flaming.

"No, no," he protested. He pulled me back. "Let me be the first," he shouted. He dropped to one knee, "Please, Marsha, let me be the first." Our friends in the room laughed and applauded, Kevin's going nuts, the guy's losing it. Only Meghan knew that something was the matter. She pushed her way over to me and shoved at Kevin.

"You shit," she hissed at him. "Let go of her right now."

"Nobody noticed, nobody noticed," she told me when she had gotten me back outside. I was crying, furious, and trying to be silent. There were still one or two couples outside, whispering from their places on trailer steps around the courtyard, walking up the paths on their way to warm beds.

"It's a lie," I told her. "He's making it up."

"It's okay." She didn't know whether to hold on to me, and I didn't know that that's what would have helped. We stayed side by side, me crying and her lying back to me, saying it was okay, that nobody had heard him, and anyway nobody believed it. Then all the lights went out in the whole trailer park, just for a few seconds, and in the sudden silence the cold seized us.

"It feels like home," I told her, "like it's going to snow tonight." But Meghan laughed and said that she had never heard of it snowing in Palo Alto.

The lights came back on an instant later. I heard friends leaving, saying their good nights. People would walk by soon; maybe Kevin would come out, still drunk, or worse, apologetic.

"I have to go," I told Meghan.

"Where?" she asked. "It's late."

"I'll be back." I ran off down the path. "Don't wait up," I called. "Don't worry."

At night they locked the doors of married student housing. I stood outside for ten long minutes until someone came by and let me in. Then I stood for another five outside Stephan's door, trying to figure out how to summon him.

"Stephan!" I called in a low whisper to the door. "Stephan!" But of course he didn't hear me. I wanted the courage to knock and demand him. I wanted to call his name and see him come hurrying out. Who gave a damn if Marcie heard me; let her come too and rouse the whole building with her angry shouts. It would make it real, to be confronted by an injured wife. I knelt in the hallway and put my ear to the door. I heard something—I pressed closer till it pained me.

"Maman!" I heard. I cursed Nikki: shut up and go to bed.

And then a man's voice, rough but laughing, and a woman's fluting reply.

"I am busy," I thought I heard her call to her child in French. "Tomorrow you can come and show me."

The boy obeyed her, as I had seen him do every time. I should have liked him better, but I have no apology for that. The child was not my interest, and adults—even women, I'm convinced—cannot always be expected to throw themselves down before a child.

Then I heard a sharp voice from behind me.

"You want Stephan, don't you?"

I turned and saw a woman standing in the doorway of the apartment across the hall. She wore a blue dressing gown, barely wrapped, and held one arm at the elbow and the other crooked as though she were flourishing a cigarette, and I was so dumb in my youth at that time, so easily shrunk by the poses of people older and harder by only a handful of years, that I pulled in my limbs and dropped my head, wanting to contract even smaller.

"Oh yes, you want Stephan," she said. "So many of them do." I wondered did she stand at her doorway at all hours, her eyeball to the tiny peephole, waiting for Stephan to walk out of his apartment or seeking to know her rivals.

"Stephan!" she called suddenly, and she strode past me to pound on his door. I put my hand up to stop her but I didn't want to touch her. Her blue robe stroked me across the face in the rhythm of her fist striking Stephan's door.

He opened the door fast and swore so easily at her that he must have known by her voice who was calling him out. It gave me heart to hear the excoriation. I wonder about that now, why I didn't see universality in his abuse, but the cold, the late hour, my rise, at last, from my crouch to a standing position must have confused me—also my desire. I let him finish with her; then I showed myself behind her, and I gave him, God help me, what I thought was a seductive smile.

"But Marsha," he said. "What are you doing here? Nikki is long ago asleep."

I came for you, I intended to say. I thought you, I thought we, when I left you told me that you sometimes got free at night—. But I didn't get the words out, and that was the one saving grace. That was the one thing I was thankful for in my deep humiliation. The Fates intervened for that one moment and spared me the degradation of speaking hope aloud, and though I know enough now to know that my shame was wasted and that I would give anything—half my life, half of all my confident moments, and more—to return to that blessed stupid innocent state, at the time this all happened, I felt relief for days that I had not uttered what was obvious to everyone.

"Stephan," called a voice, a third woman, his wife, and there was Marcie, coming up behind, a rose-colored robe to match her neighbor's blue one. Her hands flitted, her expression too, from shock to comprehension to forced amusement.

"Send your admirers home," she instructed him. Her hands ran again through her chestnut tangle. "I am going back to bed. It's chilly here in the doorway." She turned, I turned, the woman in the blue robe turned, as though we three were cued by sound or light, and we all went back the way we had come.

The cold cut through me on the dark walk home. The stars were gone, clouds had gathered. I tried to slide my hands into my jean pockets, but only a few fingers fit; the bulk of my hands bulged, unprotected. At the corner I stopped, thinking it would be safer to stay on the street, to walk down the middle, lit by the street-lamps, but instead I turned and crossed a parking lot. A woman had been murdered by her lover on campus—but it was too cold for that kind of danger tonight. I walked down the steps of a grand old dormitory and heard my own sneakered footfalls. Dead Week had begun and everyone was sleeping. They would all be asleep in the trailers too, the courtyard cleaned up, the furniture put back together, one week to go and all of us at last buckling down to work. I came around the corner and entered the trailer park. Through one courtyard, through another. I counted the trailers as I walked past.

"Two twos are four," I whispered to myself. "Three twos are six. Four twos are eight." 25W loomed before me. It sat awkwardly, seeming to sag to the left. Its front steps looked splintered and warped. I put my hand to the corner of the trailer. If I gave it a shove, maybe it would fall right over. Tip off its foundings and slide like a load off a dump truck into the dirt. I braced my other hand and pushed as hard as I could. The sky above me started swirling. I'm doing it, I thought. I'm pushing the fucking thing over. Then I heard a banging coming from the back door.

"It's snowing!" shouted Kevin. He banged the door again. "Wake up! Wake up and see this! It's snowing out here!"

My hands slipped off the corner of the trailer, my fingers red and swollen from the cold. The night was quiet except for Kevin calling. I hid one of my hands inside the warm cave of the other while the snow fell steadily around me.

Dougie

I am an expert in empty houses. I haven't paid rent in over two years. People are constantly leaving in a hurry. They have plants to water, mail to collect. They have old dogs and worried cats. They get my name from a friend of a friend, and I turn up with a tiny-sized tote—this tells them right away that I'm not an invader. I'm always surprised at how good they make me feel. Warm and trustworthy. Neighborly.

I call my brother Randy on my way into town. It's the end of the day, rush hour, and Randy I know is getting ready to work. I close the door of the phone booth and now I feel like Houdini, Houdini as a woman in a strong glass box. Even with the door shut, I have to shout to make him hear me. There didn't used to be so many cars and trucks.

"I'm back," I tell him. "I've got a new gig."

"A job?" asks Randy. He's joking, I know it. I've stayed with him a few times, between empty houses, but now he's married, and I'm self-sufficient. I haven't dropped in on him for six months running.

"A house," I say. "Right here in town." I lean against the glass; it warms my shoulder. This might be the last real phone booth in all the Garden State. "A shingled house with a yard in back. Nice big elm trees all around. Come over and see it. You'll feel right at home."

"What street?" asks Randy. Already he's suspicious. I can't fool him, but I don't really try.

I name the street. He pauses. I can't wait; I tell him the number.

"So the Jeffreys' house," he says. "Right next door to Mom."

"Janet Jeffrey took Herb to Omaha for new bone marrow."

"That's not funny, Nina. Not funny at all."

"Not the Herb part. Poor Herb. But back on the street—doesn't that give you a chuckle?"

"For how long?" he asks.

"They don't know yet. It could be weeks."

Randy changes his mind. He does that to me sometimes, but I always roll with his punches. "That's great news," he says. I switch shoulders, feel the sun-warmth spread. I wonder if the Jeffreys have lawn chairs in the backyard, so Randy and I can sit outside and smoke.

"You can help Mom," I hear him saying. "She needs company, what with Dick taking off."

I crack the door of the phone booth open.

"I can't hear you," I shout. I hold the receiver to the car-whipped wind. "Come over after work. I'll be there in an hour."

The wind blows in both directions. I can't hear him say when he'll stop by for a visit.

My mother's forearms are hinging like a hatch; she thinks she's on a runway guiding in a loaded jet. I'd rather park on the street for a quick getaway if I need it, but I like to live by certain guidelines, little principles that have seen me through. The one I'm thinking of at the moment is this: small concessions are never a waste of time. I pull my car into the Jeffreys' garage. It's better than my mother's: a car fits.

"Poor Herb," says my mother. "New bone marrow, can you imagine? They asked me to take the test, but I said no. They're not family."

This is my mother's way of telling me that if I were dying, she'd take the test. I'll save her the trouble: we'd never be a match.

She hands me the keys and Janet Jeffrey's list, "Household Instructions for Nina, Thanx so much!!" Two pages in apricot ink. My mother will be hard-pressed to improve on it.

"Herb can't be that bad off. Janet had time to write this."

"Don't forget to buy toilet paper. Janet will want you to supply your own. Paper towels. Garbage bags. Wet and dry cat food. Janet says Dougie takes both."

I look around and see Dougie lying under the kitchen table and that stuns me. Dougie's as old as I am, which is impossible, but maybe it's true. I can't wait to tell Randy. We had talked about killing off that cat a hundred times on visits to the old neighborhood. We never settled on a nice quiet way to do it.

"Who's been taking care of him?" The Jeffreys have been gone for a week.

"Jim Spinks, the middle boy across the street. He's thirteen."

It amazes me that she still knows the kids on the block. Most of the houses have changed hands more than once, and the neighbors don't talk to each other anymore, or anyway not to me. They scurry inside when they see me coming, my engine gunning, my hair wild from the wind. There's something about the set of my shoulders and the square of my hips that makes people nervous. If you can't be tall, wide is the next best thing.

Or maybe it's not the way I look. Maybe the stories about Randy and me are legendary, passed like tribal history from neighbor to neighbor, or disclosed as part of any real estate sale on the block. We did a few things in our youth. Maybe they remember all that.

My mother opens Mrs. Jeffrey's refrigerator.

"I'll be fine," I say quickly. I want her to go home. "I'll just settle in"—I wave my apricot pages—"and bone up." My mother sighs and edges out the door. She doesn't offer casserole; such is the reach of my luck.

When I get back from the 7-Eleven, I turn out the lights and wait. I know she's waiting too, sitting in her living room with her plants and my father's plaster globe. It's a relief map of the world, with ridges for mountain ranges and bumps for tiny islands that Randy called nips on a titty. I checked my own the night he told me that. They were just coming out, ugly, unwanted. Various men have praised them since, but I never did get the praise I wanted from Randy. I tried a few times—I was ten or maybe more. Fourteen maybe; I can't say exactly, but I know I had something under my shirt to show him. He was interested for a while—I remember his interest—until one day he told me to knock it off and he hit me. Not a hard slap, more like a friendly punch. After that, it was strictly boy stuff between us, like we had been brothers or teammates all along. If he came over tonight and made that joke again, if he compared those islands to my grown-up bruiser bumps, or squeezed me hard, the way he used to, I'd scream with laughter like when we were kids. I'd let him sock me a punch if he wanted to. The globe itself is worthless. It names a lot of countries that don't exist anymore.

I pick up the phone and call Randy again.

"The hell I will," he says. All I've asked is, drive your pickup over and let's clean Dick's stuff out of Mom's garage. He was a great one for equipment, Dick. Ride-on mower, jigsaw, a two-hose vac for my mother's Buick. He left it all behind when he took off, handing my mother his Costco card. Dad's pension will pay till she's gone. She didn't need Dick for the money.

"Just get it hauled away," says Randy. He's got a bar on the other side of town—a sports bar with big-screen TVs and a decent steak off the grill. "I've got better things to do."

"It might be worth something. There might be a few hundred bucks just sitting there. That mower, for instance. The clubs. You can't see Mom needing those clubs."

"The clubs are gone. I took the clubs."

"You took the clubs?"

"I've been playing."

"Where?"

"Muni course. Just nine holes," he says, and I hear that note in his voice, that funny little note. He's done that to me before. You might call it an apology, but then again.

"Just the nine holes," my brother says to me.

"Help me get that mower started."

"The hell I will."

My mother gives up around eleven. Hard to tell, the way her house is lit up, but at eleven, the bedroom lights go low, and I begin to move around.

I don't need light. The Jeffreys' house is my mother's, flipped. Our kitchen, their laundry. Our dining room, their stairs. Only the upstairs bathroom is different. The Jeffreys put in bright blue tile and a long skylight over the tub. That surprises me, for no good reason. A customized bathroom should not throw me for a loop.

I go back downstairs and sit in the living room, away from the window on the street. There are china rabbits on the side tables but no ashtray in sight. I light a joint, take a hit, tap the ash into the palm of my hand. I smoke it down, but the high comes on slow. The days and nights have slowed like that for me. Where everything used to move fast, there are long minutes of stillness. You ought to appreciate that, I say aloud. Everybody else is out looking for that kind of peace. Randy out there on the golf course, swinging the irons, he's looking for a big comfy chair in the Jeffreys' living room, smoking down the butt. I fall asleep sitting there, cupping the ash like a handful of gold.

The next morning, Jim Spinks comes by to feed Dougie. I invite him to come in and give him a drink of water.

"I've got the cat now," I tell Jimmy Spinks. "Mrs. Jeffrey left me instructions."

The boy lights up like a Christmas candle.

"Great," he says. "I don't like that cat. Look what it did." He holds out his hand. His arm is thin and barely freckled. His T-shirt hangs from his shoulder like a cape. I see three long scratches down the back of his hand, scabbed in little beads like poison ivy.

"I know that cat," I tell him. I'm still a little high from the night before so I walk around the kitchen, not wanting the boy to see. "He's a very sneaky cat."

Jimmy Spinks looks interested. I don't know kids, but I've been told they like a story.

"My brother, Randy, and I used to live next door. So one time, Mrs. Jeffrey asked us to take care of Dougie while they were gone for the weekend."

I check his glass and get him more water.

"The first night we came over to feed him, he jumped onto the kitchen counter, right over there, where Mrs. Jeffrey kept a bowl of pinecones and nuts."

"Pinecones and nuts?"

I nod and get up to check. There it is, maybe the same bowl. I show it to Jimmy; he picks up a pecan and tries to crack it with his teeth.

"So Dougie jumped up there and started playing with the nuts. Randy told him to cut it out. The cat didn't listen. So Randy swatted him down, not hard, just a sweep and a swat, to get him off the counter. He took a walnut with him."

"The cat took a walnut?"

"He wanted to play with it. He rolled it down there and back," I point to the hallway, "and in there too." I get up and walk across the hall to the living room, and Jimmy follows. The Jeffreys have hardwood floors in their living room, something else that's different. They have honey oak floors with the high-gloss finish. My mother has Stainmaster.

"Dougie rolled the walnut from one end of the room to the other. It made a big racket. He kept rolling it back and forth, so Randy took it away from him, put it back in the bowl, put the bowl in the kitchen cabinet."

Jimmy Spinks nods twice, maybe three times. I'm telling a good story, and it happens to be true.

"The next day when we came back, Dougie had the walnut again. He was rolling it all over the living room, batting it back and forth between his paws. We couldn't figure out where he had got it. We checked the kitchen—the cabinet door was shut tight. We looked all around the house for another bowl of nuts, but—nothing."

"Then what?"

"I chased Dougie under the couch and went to pick up the walnut." I lean forward, like I'm scooping up a nut. I raise my fingers to see what I've got and make a magnificent face. "The walnut had whiskers! And two little black eyes looking straight at me!" I throw nothing down to the floor and jump back from Jimmy with a flourish.

"Where was the rest of it?" Jimmy wants to know.

"Randy disposed of it."

"Disposed of it?"

I push my tits together with the both of my hands. Jimmy Spinks sees but doesn't comment.

"He put it in the trash," I tell him.

"That's what I would have done," says Jimmy Spinks.

I move my hands to the boy's thin shoulders. "Then you're a smart kid." He looks a little nervous—my wideness again—and leaves the house without finishing his water.

My mother comes over after Jimmy Spinks leaves.

"You had talents," she tells me. "The same as your brother. I want to remind you of that."

"I'm perfectly happy. I don't need more." I hold my voice steady so she'll have to believe, but she shakes her head, leaning on Mrs. Jeffrey's kitchen counter. It's identical to my mother's, green and yellow with metal trim. I imagine we're standing in my mother's kitchen, having our familiar chat.

I want to tell her that I've missed nothing out of life, and it's not my fault that she's alone and old. But what's the point of saying it, when it's so obviously true? My mother is as old as the house we stand in, as old as the house next door, while I'm out in the world, not in need of anything she's got left to offer. The sunlight's coming in strong. I can see the ridges of age in her face, like the surface of the globe she won't throw away, or the shell of a hard brown nut.

"What are you going to do with your life?" she asks. "Tell me that. What are you going to do?"

I left two boxes in my mother's garage. It was the safest place I had to store them, but I wonder now if my mother threw them out. A picture of my parents, my grandmother's shawl. A magic book that Randy gave me which described step-by-step how to stage an amazing escape. The book kept me busy for one whole summer, and that's another little rule that's served me through the years: if you look busy, people leave you alone.

I lean and kiss my mother's wrinkles.

"I have plans," I tell her. "All sorts of projects I'm going to accomplish."

She shakes her head. "You don't know what you're missing," she says. "You should stand right there and figure it out."

I wave to her and walk out of the kitchen. I remember to turn left instead of right as I head down the hall. I think my mother might forget she's in Janet Jeffrey's house and stand there until I come back. But she doesn't. She finds her way home.

After she's gone, I return to the kitchen. I wasn't lying to my mother. I've hit on a project, a little challenge to make the time pass. I crouch down to the lower cabinets. I'm looking for something tall that can take water and a pipe. Out in computerland, people are talking to each other about how to make a bomb. Here in Janet Jeffrey's kitchen, it's Bong Construction 101.

In the third cabinet to the right of the sink, I find a plastic measuring cup with a long spout sticking out near the bottom. The box calls it a gravy strainer, and that's a new one on me. The fat—the smoke—is supposed to rise to the top. The good stuff stays on the bottom.

I can't find another strainer so I settle for a piece of the Jeffreys' screen door, a three-quarters-inch circle near the bottom. I poke the piece of screen halfway down the spout. It makes a snug little shelf. "For keeping us high and dry," I tell the screen, as I back out my pinky. "That's your job. That's all I require."

The thumbhole is trickier. I've got a drill from Herb's workbench, but the bit is bigger than I want. I set the tip a few inches below the lip of the strainer, halfway around between the spout and the handle. It's good, strong plastic. It lets the bit right through without cracking. I blow away the dustings, test my thumb over the hole. Then I go out to enjoy the sunshine. Randy and I will test my handiwork tonight.

In the evening, after my mother drives off to meet a girlfriend for bridge or a movie, I head over to Randy's place. I drive slowly to make sure I don't get there before he does. His truck is there, not Miss Ann's. She's probably at home, sewing curtains. I park in her spot, next to Randy. If she comes and sees her spot taken, maybe she'll turn around and go right back home.

I plan to walk in and pound the bar, demand a cold one before he turns around. But he's just outside the doorway, checking out the lot. He might have been watching when I climbed out of my car. I changed my shirt before I came and tucked the tails into my jeans. Not to meet somebody, not here, at Randy's. But appearances concern him; I've seen that in recent years. I blame Miss Ann. He says it's business.

"Did you ask Mom to come with you?" I don't get a hug, but he does pat my shoulder.

I say quickly, "She had plans."

He cocks his head and gives me a look. He's wearing his old red plaid shirt, but underneath, a blue shirt with pearly buttons. Two-thirds of his beard is gone; there's only the bristle around his mouth, like a basket holding a pair of lips. He's got new glasses—my brother, Ben Franklin, checking me over from the tip of his nose.

"Let's get you a steak," he says. He pulls off his plaid shirt and heads inside. I start to follow, but he turns back quickly, so I have to pull up short. I see copper hairs like clipped wire in his beard. There's hardly a smell of smoke about him.

"No cigarettes anymore in the bar," he tells me.

"But I'm a regular," I joke.

"Even I go outside." He points to the doorway. "People nowadays. They go right out and report you."

"You shouldn't have added food," I say, though that was two

years ago. Mom lent him the money. "Before food, you didn't attract that kind of trash."

He laughs, so I show him that I'm putting my cigarettes away, zipping them into an inside pocket. My jacket is thin; I can feel the packet rubbing against my left nipple. I might say something later about the effect, though for now, I save it. Ammunition for Miss Ann.

He tells the waitress to bring me a steak and a beer, and I see her eyes flick at my chopped brown hair, at my dusty boots. She's leaning a little closer than necessary to hear what Randy's saying. I try to catch his eye, meaning to roll mine, but he's busy straightening, stepping back from the girl. She's dumb anyway, doesn't see the family resemblance, or she'd ask me, draught or bottle, and how do I want it cooked. Randy puts his hand on my elbow; I slide into a booth.

"Mom good?" he asks.

I nod. "She's fine." I mock her look and his. "She's at me again—you'd think she'd be glad to see me. Coming home to pay my respects."

Randy frowns. "She's feeling pretty bad for Herb and Janet." He chews a few pretzels. I check out the bowl. No walnuts in there, just pretzels and crackers, powdered orange. "She say anything about Dick?" he asks.

"I forgot to ask." His beard dips; the eyeglasses too. If he's so pissed at the man, why not help me find a buyer for his stuff?

"What makes a man do something like that?" asks Randy. "What makes him just pick up and leave?" He shakes his head; he doesn't expect an answer, but then he looks right at me, and I see that he does. "Just pick up and leave," he says. "Why would a man do that?"

Well it's true that I've had some experience on the subject. That I've had a few men just pick up on me and leave. But I've never traced that back to a reason, and if I could find one, I wouldn't bring it up with Randy. We have our history, and that's been enough for me. Except now he's asking, torn up for Mom.

"I admire Dick," I reply. "Light on his feet, after all those years." Dick was square and wide—maybe I was thinking of me.

Randy pushes at the pretzels in disgust. He looks around. The bar is getting noisy; business is coming in.

I tell him, "It's a virtue, being light on your feet."

"I don't know about that," says Randy. He looks around again; he's reluctant to stay talking.

"Guess what," I say. "Do you remember Dougie? Mrs. Jeffrey's cat? He's still around. I'm taking care of him now."

"Dougie," says Randy. He stops to marvel, just like I did. "I remember that cat." He starts to laugh. "I remember getting him high."

"In our backyard. He came over to hunt insects after dark. You tried calling him, but he didn't trust you."

"I grabbed that cat," says Randy. He's demonstrating now, his thick arms bulging. "Blew the smoke right down his gullet."

"And Mom wanted to know what happened to your face."

"And Mrs. Jeffrey told her the next day that Dougie had eaten twice his normal ration." We're laughing together, hearing our mother excited to tell the tale. I want to reach over to him when we laugh together like this, but I leave my hands on the table and settle instead for his grin.

"Come over tonight," I say. "I've got some good stuff. We can share it with Dougie."

He shakes his head. "Can't tonight."

I don't answer, so he knocks his right knuckles against my hands. We're both looking at his knuckles, like they're about to speak, and I let go my grin now, my fingers stiffening in their curl. I've been like this always, waiting, waiting. I watch his hand slide slowly away until it disappears under the table.

"So anyway," he says. He clears his throat. "Ann's coming in later. Stick around and say hi."

The steak arrives. He leaves me to it.

Miss Ann comes in as I'm finishing my beer. She's wearing jeans too, only hers end above her ankles so she can show her white feet. Randy kisses her, and she stands with him for a second, sweeping her gaze around the bar to check up on how everything looks. She doesn't look my way, though she knows I'm here. Randy's whispering to her now, stroking her hair. I see her give him a brave smile. Then she shakes her head at his old plaid shirt draped over the chair at the front. She pulls it off the chair and heads toward me, bundling up the shirt in her hands. There's no flesh on the woman, only springy muscle, and that's how I think of her, bouncing like an itty ball, the tiny pink ones the girls used for playing jacks while the boys grappled with each other in the dirt. She moves briskly, but I'm not impressed. It's not the same as light on the feet.

"It's nice to see you," she says, sliding into the booth. Randy is watching us. I don't believe her for a second.

"The place looks good." I wave to Randy; he waves back. His eyes look squinched behind his glasses. "And busy," I add. Randy greets more people coming in.

"The dinner crowd starts about now." Miss Ann gives me a look. There are eight booths, and I'm in the best one.

I lean back, stretch my legs. "What's different about the place? Something seems different."

"I had the shutters replaced. And the lights in front are new." With me leaning back, Miss Ann leans forward. It feels like a seesaw, one up, one down. I want to see her dangle, white feet kicking.

"You should do the same for Mom," I say. "The Jeffreys' house looks a lot better than hers."

Miss Ann pinches her lips together. Her face looks white too. She's clutching Randy's shirt in front of her stomach; then she notices what she's doing and puts the shirt aside. Hands on her stomach. Her pale pale face. Tits as big as mine now, where before she had nothing. A little speculation works its way into my head, and of course I have to test it. She's looking around for some place to focus, so I push my dinner dishes right under her nose. My heavy glass, with its thick ring of beer foam, my swabbed plate with its pile of gristle. She swallows hard and starts to retch.

"You going to be sick?" I ask her. I push the plate even closer.

"Oh god," says Miss Ann. "Take that thing away."

"What have you done," I tell her. "You've gone and got yourself pregnant? It's a bad idea. It's an all-around terrible plan. Randy hates babies. And he beats up on girls. He ever tell you that?"

Her heaving stops. She sits back in the booth.

"Shut up," she says. I see her hand, as white as her pretty feet, wiping itself across her bright pink mouth.

"He used to beat me up," I say. "He'd do anything to get his hands on me. Once there was this dead mouse." I open my shirt by a couple of buttons. "He put it down my shirt. Just slipped it right down there"—I shove three fingers down—"and when I started screaming, he went looking for it again."

"Get out," says Randy. He's got an arm wrapped around his wife, and she's crying, telling him I'm a monster.

"You did those things to me," I answer him.

"Come on, come on," he says, pulling me by the arm and hauling me out the door. I drag my feet like the old days, putting up just enough resistance to keep the game going.

"Go on home," says Randy. He opens my car door.

"You come with me."

"No."

I want to hit him in the face. I want him to touch me. I lean in, he pulls back, and now I'm the one dangling.

"You used to," I say.

"We were kids," says Randy. "Will you just forget about it? It was stupid stuff, and it should have ended earlier. But for Christ's sake, I wish you'd leave it."

I hit him anyway, a tad more than a friendly punch.

"You should forget it," he says again. When he walks away, I look down at my fists. One is holding on to that plaid shirt of Randy's, and the other starts to pull on it like it's tied to something safe.

My mother is still out when I get home. I wait for a while in Janet Jeffrey's kitchen. Then I go to my mother's garage, to see what all was left behind.

There are tools on the workbench; I put those aside right away, but other than that, I can't get to a thing. The junk and the valuables are jumbled together, nothing boxed or hung up on hooks. I spy the mower under a pile of metal—old bikes, a clothesline pole, an empty gas tank. I can't get close to the mower unless I move all the rest of it out of the way. My own two boxes are nowhere to be seen. They've disappeared like magic. I'd like to do that kind of magic, to wave my hand, make the past go away. The dust is thick;

I don't want to touch it. Goddamned Randy. He pawed through here and left the place a mess. I pull my knees high making my way back out. I don't want to trip on a single goddamned thing.

I go back next door and call for Dougie, but he won't come, so I start without him. He'll come running when he smells good shit.

My kitchenware handiwork looks even better tonight. I trickle in the water, stopping just before the spout. The weed I push until it rests against the screen. I get it lit and glue my face to the cup. I suck. The smoke swirls. I have to suck hard; my efficiencies are off because the cup is wide and the spout oddly angled, but I'm used to making do. When I take my thumb off the hole I drilled, the smoke shoots into me, the breath of life.

I finish and go looking for Dougie. He's not in the dining room, the bedrooms, or the bathroom. He hasn't been at his food or water all day. I go back to the kitchen and sort through the bowl of pinecones and nuts. He's not under the radiator or behind the living room couch. I make little cat noises and go out into the night.

It's almost dark, and a shadowy moon is rising through the pin oaks and sycamore trees. No one walks by. I think about asking Jimmy Spinks to lend a hand, but I don't trust myself to get past his mother. I put my head back, sweep my eyes through the trees. The Jeffreys have good, big trees—elms alongside the sycamores and a dogwood next to the house. I hear Dougie calling me from far above—he's stuck somewhere, I instantly know it. Stuck in a place he shouldn't have tried to go.

He's up on the roof, a little peaked part that sticks out over the dormer to the middle bedroom. I map it in my mind, flipping it as I scramble. That was Randy's room. In our house, you could climb out that dormer window all the way to the roof. Randy had nailed a crosspiece a few feet above the sill, a foothold to get up and back down. From the sill to the foothold, and the foothold to the dormer roof. From there to the main roof, where he would inch along on his stomach, looking down on the world. He never wanted me to follow, so I watched him from the window or took his orders down on the lawn. I went up by myself once or twice after he left. I couldn't find the point in it, since he wasn't there to see it.

Now that I've spotted him, Dougie is really starting to yowl. I sprint up the stairs to the bedroom, open the window, and lift out the screen. He swishes his tail; he's happy to see me. I can't rescue myself, but I can do something for Dougie. And I'll have a good story to tell Jimmy Spinks. That cat and me, we go way back. He's practically like a brother.

"Good boy, Dougie. I'm a-comin'."

The window frame is in good shape, not loose with age like my mother's. I ease myself up and out the window. As I raise my whole body, Dougie jumps to the main roof above. He crouches there, yowling. I see his fear. I can smell it.

"Kitty, kitty, kitty." I wave my arm, but Dougie's too scared to come back down, and how would he do it if he wanted. I'm strong. I can do it, even without Randy's crosspiece. I brace my foot and power up. I make the dormer roof, no problem.

In the old days, Randy would stand on the peak of the dormer roof and lean against the main roof, which was not all that steep. One leg swung up would gain him the ridge. I do it just like that, aiming for a spot behind Dougie.

But the peak of the roof is sharper than I remember, or maybe I've got more belly to drape. It didn't seem so high a moment ago, from the sill. The hind end of Dougie is inches from my face. I reach a hand to grab him. With a second swish of his ratty gray tail, he jumps back down to the dormer roof and disappears through the open bedroom window. He's laughing, I know it, and Jimmy Spinks will laugh at me too.

I swear a couple of times, but I don't let myself lose it. I'm trying to hang on to another one of my theories: if you keep an even surface, the mess underneath can't reach up and grab you. I hump along the ridge, thinking how to signal. I'm not going to start yelling, but waving seems all right. I'm headed for the chimney stack. With one arm, I'll hold on to the chimney; with the other, I'll try a big wave. I'm strong. I know how to balance.

A few feet below and to the side of the chimney stack, skylight glass bulges, pale against the shingled roof. I sit up and put one hand on the corner of the red brick chimney, bracing my left foot against the frame of the skylight. My right foot I set at the ridge-line of the roof. I stand. I look out from the Jeffreys' rooftop into the street below.

The Buick drives up; my mother gets out. She walks holding

her elbows, with her sweater draped so it swings from her shoulders like a bell. In the moonlight, I see her hair and her hands. I cannot see her face.

"Mom," I call down from the rooftop. She looks up at me. I wave.

"Now can you see," she calls back. Her face is shining like a girl awaiting a kiss. "Now can you see what you're missing?"

"Take me at my word," I call down to my mother. "I've got everything I ever wanted."

I lift one knee high, then the other, ready to show her I could walk off into the air. My feet are as light as smoke. My face is grinning. But something not myself pulls my arms around the chimney, and though I want to, I can't let go.

The
Long
Way
Home

No one in my family knows it was me who set the fire. I did it deliberately, meaning this: I made a loose pile of my sister's eight most precious things—one for each year I bore her existence—struck a match and coaxed forth a blaze. I was eight years old; my sister Joanna was ten. I didn't know the house would go. The beds, the sofa, the green glass plates my mother used to serve cake. But I knew the match would lead to fire, and fire to destruction of possessions held dear. I was not so sorry watching it all happen. I was sorry later, the next twenty-one years.

My parents think it started at a faulty closet light. I will tell them today how it really happened. I have chosen today as carefully as I cupped my hand and blew, delivering my message with one long, giving breath. The paper caught, the fabric too. They will learn all about it at five o'clock.

It's warm and sunny, a good day for confession.

"I'm here," I call as I head up the walkway to my parents' second house. My father won't remember that I told them I would visit, but my mother looks out the window, waves a happy hand. They live in the flats, in a two-bedroom box built to match its neighbors. Not as nice as their first house, but still—says my father, when anyone complains—a house. A house.

"He's wonderful today," my mother tells me. "His old self." She forgave him years ago, six weeks after his own tearful confession; since then, she looks for signs of the man she forced herself to absolve.

"Look, Dad." I hold up from my shopping bag a fat triangle of brie. His doctors have forbidden it, making it all the more worthy of his lust.

"Plenty ripe I hope," he says. He's sniffing at the package like a dog.

"Oozing," I assure him. He smacks his drooping lips. For my mother I've brought coffee beans and chocolates and embroidery needles I've already threaded in fifteen different shades of orange and red. She's working on a sunset. "Southwestern," she informed me, "for the little pillow on Dad's old chair." I imagine the outline of one noble cactus and layers of color indicating sky.

These are not bribes or offerings of peace. It is part of my job to supply delectables; I've been doing so now for more than ten years. Joanna brings her troubles, and I bring the bounty. A husband, five years older, and a promise of grandchildren in one or two years. Words of assurance on health and money; even money itself, when my parents need it. I work as a bookkeeper. I've learned accountability and caution.

"Joanna's coming." My mother has settled into her chair, under the only decent lamp in the room. I'm fetching her needlework; with my back to her, I make an extravagant face.

"I thought she was away. In Oregon or something." I'm not all that surprised. My sister has a taste for drama, a sixth sense for spectacle and final acts. She's discovered two suicides and seen a boy drown.

My mother pulls the lamp closer. She spreads her needlework

over her bulbous knees. She's got skinny legs and feet that slip into girls' buckle sandals, but her knees look huge, the caps like eggshells waiting to be cracked.

"Oh you girls," she says. I'm dismayed to hear her mantra spoken with more humor than grief. Once our battles were my mother's greatest sorrow. Joanna would hate as much as I to have become a source of gentle exasperation, or worse yet, amusement.

"Well I'm glad she's coming," I tell my mother, but already she's bent over the array of needles I've brought her, the gleam of gluttony brightening her eyes. She chooses one threaded in pale orange and slides it into her needlework with an addict's ecstasy. In the kitchen I hear my father snuffling cheese; here in the living room, my mother's swooning. Be content with the little things in life. It's practical advice, glossed by modesty and a hint of devotion. My father quotes it like scripture to anyone dull enough to listen. I've taken up the cause, embraced it as my own. Where would I be without the little things? Eight little things brought me here. I could name you each if I had to.

It's four thirty; I could call my father in and tell them outright, but that isn't the way I've got it planned. I perch on the love seat wedged between my parents' chairs. I want to wait until five, which is the time it happened, while my mother was getting supper and Joanna was walking home from Trisha Blume's house. Ritual should be part of confession, memory part of penance.

"Do you remember Trish Blume?" I ask my mother. She nods right away; she lives better in the beforetime, unencumbered by The Tragedy and Dad's Big Mistake.

"Joanna's friend," says my mother. "She played the piano, something you girls wouldn't do."

"I looked her up once. She wasn't in the phone book, and the school couldn't find her."

"She was two years ahead of you."

"I liked her," I say.

"No you didn't." She jerks the needle; is she peeved at me, my fatuous declaration, or at the thread, snarled like fishing line on a treacherous branch? I'm relieved to hear her annoyance; this is the mother I've known and loved.

"She was friendly when Joanna wasn't around."

"Harry," calls my mother. She has to call twice before my father hears. "Come away from that cheese, you've had enough." He shuffles into the room, his gums still working. He once was tall and carried his stoutness forward; now his spine bends him over like a firm hand on the back of his neck. I am short, like my mother, but I have sturdy legs and strong, square shoulders. I share a face with Joanna—wide cheekbones, blunt brow. In family pictures, only Joanna and I look related.

"Susie is asking about Trisha Blume." My father nods and creaks into his chair.

"A nice girl," says my father. He motions for me to bring him his paper. "You were all sweethearts. Joanna, Susie, and Trish."

"Remember that Joanna was at Trisha's the night of the fire?" My father frowns at his paper; my mother covers her mouth.

"Why bring that up?" She drops her hand, starts smoothing her knees again, ironing out the past. "Why bring that up at a time like this?"

"No one was hurt, because Joanna was at Trisha's. That was lucky, don't you think?"

"You were hurt," says my mother. I have six-inch patches of grafted skin on the inside of my forearms. They are shiny but flesh-colored. When I put lotion on, they polish up and glisten. My sweater caught as I was jumping for the door.

"I forget they're even there." I tuck my wrists behind, though my arms are clothed in cotton.

"Three skin grafts," says my mother, disbelieving. She raises her voice. "Insurance paid for that, thank God. Otherwise we never could have managed."

My father opens his paper, sticks his head inside. I'm sorry she brought it up, but I knew it might happen. I'll make it better in a minute; it's almost five o'clock. Mother forgave him but can't resist exposing him from time to time. They had no insurance on the house. My mother called, screamed at the agent. Policy canceled, he kept on repeating, until finally she put down the phone. A year of premiums had gone unpaid. It took them six years to pay back the bank, another five to make a down payment. They borrowed money from her parents, and my mother took work as a bookkeeper's assistant.

The back door bangs; it's Joanna. I realize I've been hoping she'll get here in time. She kisses Mother, gives Dad a rough pat.

"You never use the front door," says my mother mildly.

"Sand," she replies, holding up her shoes. She's been at the beach; her dark hair is tangled. She carries their house key loose in her pocket. Has she lost her bag again or was her van broken into? No doubt another roommate has ripped her off. She shoves the key back into her pocket and appraises me.

"You look fancy," she says. I took extra effort before I left my house. My same dark hair is smoothed back with a band; my shoes are polished, and I'm wearing a soft skirt.

"I'm glad you're here. I have something to say."

"Before I have a beer?"

"Let me just say it, then you can drink," but Joanna ignores me, heads for the kitchen.

"It's cocktail hour," she calls back. The refrigerator opens and slams. I count to twenty, then twenty-five. She reappears with the beer, crackers, and the rest of Dad's brie. She eats standing up, balancing her beer on a chipped plate.

I try again. "I have something I've been wanting to say." The room feels warmer than it did ten minutes ago. I have to go to the kitchen and get a glass of water. I'm determined to keep going, to get through what I've planned. We are ready for the relief of truth. Ready to speak it, ready to receive. I'm glad Joanna is here. For all my practicing, I'll only be able to do this once. I'm sorry, I mean to tell them. They'll have to forgive me; I've been atoning all these years.

"Are you all right?" asks my mother when I come back into the room. "She's been talking about the strangest things."

"About me?" Joanna smirks, tilts the beer bottle over my head.

"No, your father," says my mother, "and his silly old mistake."

"God, Susan." Joanna straightens the beer bottle, takes a drink. "That's tacky."

"Mother brought it up, not me."

"You feed him cheese, you dig up the past. Dad," says my sister. "She's trying to kill you."

I take a breath. I see my mother's spotted hands busy with her needle.

"But don't worry," Joanna continues, "I'll light a candle for you tonight. One for Mother, two for Dad."

"You, at church?" Joanna is looking straight at me, licking her fingers like she's tugging off a glove.

"No." She's smiling. "In my tub." I kick myself; I've been in her bathroom, seen the claw-footed bathtub and dozens of candles scattered about.

"Say what?" says my father, emerging from his newspaper. He sniffs the air again, his whiskers twitching. I see my mother's lip curl; Joanna freezes. We're all watching him in faint disgust, expecting a tongue or a rough, greedy pant.

"Go on, go on." He's wagging his head, congenial and forgiving. "You're all my sweethearts, my three good girls."

They look at me, waiting, and then the penny drops. My head is halved: the brain floats; the mouth turns to lead. I want to scream but I can't; I've gone silent after years of plugging up. Were I my mother, I'd release my famous furies. A champion, my mother, at sudden attack. She would choose without pattern—Joanna, my father, or me—and begin her assessment in a clear, staccato voice. Too noisy, too quiet, too quarrelsome, and then there's your father, only good for sowing sand. Righteousness turned to shouting, shouting turned to spew. We held very still throughout the barrage; sudden movement, we figured, might bring a hard slap. She never hit Joanna or me, but once we saw her fling a dish. Dad ducked, unnecessarily. She threw like a girl of her generation. The dish hit the window and shattered them both.

"The night of the fire," I finally begin. Joanna perks up, steps closer.

"I've been thinking about how it happened."

"It's ancient history," my mother sighs. My father looks at me mournfully. I see his shoulders slump, but his sad little act doesn't reach me. I've paid his penance, more than he's paid mine.

"Joanna said she was coming home from Trisha's. Remember that? The long way home?"

"I was," says Joanna.

"But no one saw you or knew where you were."

"I came through the woods. To the back door."

"We were in front." I'm telling my parents. "Joanna came from the house when she joined us in the front yard."

"I went right through the house. In the back door, out the front." She's watching me, fascinated; so am I. My story is unraveling like a good intention, finding new form in the telling, and the telling itself is bringing me such pleasure, pleasure not known for twenty-one years.

"She said you were lucky," my mother comments. "Just a little bit earlier, she was saying how much luck."

"I think she did it," I say. "I think Joanna was in the house the whole time, that she lit a fire in our closet and couldn't put it out. I found matches in her snap wallet, hidden in her purse."

"That's priceless," says Joanna.

"We don't need to talk about this, do we?" Even in a chair, my father can't straighten. "Do we, Susie?" He rubs his head with a clumsy paw. He spent the insurance money at the track, the secret nest egg that never hatched. All of it? screamed Mother. All of the money, gone like that? Dad beat his head with softened fists. The horses, oh Jesus. Every one of them let me down.

"I'll tell you what," says Mother. I hear the bite and feel a flutter. I look to Joanna, but she looks away from me. Don't leave the room, I silently pray. She doesn't. Neither of us ever turned our back on our mother, even when we were old enough to walk away.

"Here's my heart." Mother pats the arm of her chair. "Here's all of you." She jabs in a needle and gives it a twist. "Susie. Joanna. Dad. Susie. Joanna. Dad." Every name gets a needle, every needle gets a twist. Mother is screaming by the time she's finished, and Dad is curled, his head to his knees.

"Are you happy?" asks Joanna. She's looking again, straight at me. Oh I am. I am. I knew my mother would come to my rescue. She and anger are dear old friends.

"Calm down," Joanna says to Mother. "Take a breath." Mother does, gulping air. Joanna talks to her, bringing her back. She picks up Mother's sewing, which has fallen to the floor.

"You girls," says my mother, not angry anymore, but not amused either. Joanna smoothes the sewing across our mother's lap. Only the little things demand their attention. Mother selects a needle from the studded arm of her chair.

"See to your father," she tells Joanna. She can't keep out the disdain, but Dad doesn't notice; he's still bent and curled.

"Come on, Dad." Joanna lifts him from his chair and points him toward the kitchen.

"I'm sorry," sobs my father. "I'm still so sorry I did it." Words I meant to utter and screams I meant to shout. Joanna walks, one arm at his shoulders, another at his waist. I hear her coax him with something to eat.

I stay where I am on the love seat. The story I told has closed me down like a box. My mother glows beneath her lamp, the righteous woman at her needle. If I were to slide my hands up my arms, I could finger ancient scars, but to move, to touch, would admit to what I've done. Nothing will happen if I sit very still.

Joanna makes supper, and the three of them eat. I can hear Joanna's voice, instructional and low. After dark, she sends our parents up to bed. The water runs in the kitchen, drawers are opened, plates scraped. Joanna finishes the dishes and comes into the room. My mother switched off her lamp when Joanna called her to the kitchen, so I'm in the dark, sitting.

"You were right about the matches," says Joanna. She's brought a bottle of wine and two glasses. She pours and hands me a glass. Shoves it right into my face so I have to take it.

"'Blume's the Best,'" she says. "From Trisha's father's restaurant."

"Two books," I say.

"Trish and I used to smoke his cigarettes. In the woods, taking the long way home."

"I never tried a cigarette. Not the whole time I was a child."

"You were so good," says Joanna. She moves to Mother's chair, snaps on the light. She's sitting where Mother sat, but she doesn't look anything like her. I find I can move my feet and turn my head. I hold the glass stiffly and watch Joanna drink.

"You're not happy anymore, are you?" asks Joanna.

I shake my head, no.

"It only lasts a moment," she says. "Then it goes."

I feel a giving way, at the jawline, in the knees. My shoulders drop, and my belly loosens. Not the relief I came for tonight, but my mouth is mine again, my hands set free. I lower the glass to the coffee table. Joanna leans forward and stares into my face.

"You have a lot to tell me," she says. "I think you'll do it."

I touch my sister's shoulder, but it isn't enough, so I leave the love seat, crouch in front of her chair. I lean till my forehead is pressed to Joanna's chin. It rests there for a second. We both pull back.

"Drink up," says Joanna. "It's cocktail hour somewhere in the world."

Had I been asked at my conception whether I wanted a sister at all, I would have answered truthfully, No thank you, Lord, let me be. Look what the Lord brought me, against my fervent wishes: a mother for anger, a father for tears. And a sister, Lord, for the weals of love. Delivereth my balm, a burning branch.

Gratitude

Gwen Rattle looked good when she opened the door, better than Mabel expected. She was in a black skirt and high-collared blouse. Her dark hair was bobbed short and pinned on one side with a silver clip. Mabel had tucked her own thinning hair under a small felt hat. She must have a job, thought Mabel, or family. Mabel tried to see past her shoulder. Curtains, pictures, a well-lit room. Even Mrs. Rattle had a place to call home.

"Where's Mr. Fong? Didn't he come with you?" Mabel hadn't told her on the phone that C.K. was gone. She knew it wasn't quite nice to let Mrs. Rattle think that help was at hand, but it was only a twenty-four hour lie. Mabel had told lies that lasted far longer than that. She had told Wendell, for instance, that he could do anything he set his mind to, when she knew by the time he was eight that there were many things he couldn't do. He chose sales, thank goodness, and managed that just fine.

"How do you do, Mrs. Rattle. May I come in?" Mabel smiled politely. They sat in Gwen's kitchen; she didn't offer a cup of tea.

"My son is coming home from school in twenty minutes. I don't want him to hear us talking about his dad."

"Doesn't he know his father's in—?" She almost said "the joint," and suppressed a laugh. Too many American movies late at night! C.K. had loved to watch them, sitting upright on the living room couch when he should have been struggling, like Mabel was, to fall asleep. His favorites were the old prison films about corrupt wardens and wrongly accused men. Mabel would scold him, importune him to come to bed, remind him of his morning appointments. The next day when she called to make his apologies, she would keep her voice low so that C.K. could sleep. She looked again at Gwen Rattle sitting stiffly in her chair. She knew something of that pride. Cheer up, Mrs. Rattle, she wanted to say, I'm not really here to help.

"He knows," said Gwen. "Is your husband going to take Robbie's case?"

"I'm sorry, but my husband can't help you. He died six years ago," said Mabel. She had thought Gwen might be a hairdresser or a waitress, but her hands looked as smooth as chicken breast cut from the bone.

Gwen stared. "Why didn't you tell me yesterday, when you called?"

"I didn't want to say so on the phone."

"For God's sake." Gwen stood. Mabel's veiny hands were in her lap; she gave Gwen another glimpse of her modest expression. An old Chinese lady, no harm in that.

"It's not like Robbie isn't always getting slammed by the lawyers he writes to for help anyway."

"Oh, does he send a lot of those letters?" Mabel was disappointed for C.K.

Gwen sat back down. "Yeah, I tell him not to waste the stamps. They got him in there now, why let him out early? Most of those guys he writes to don't even bother to write back. They see it's jail mail and throw it away."

"What did he do?" asked Mabel.

"He's *accused* of mugging a guy, taking him down with The Club." She shook her head. "We don't even own a car."

"C.K. never practiced law, but he had legal training and many good *ideas*," said Mabel.

"For God's sake. Your husband, who's dead, never handled a case? Why did you bother to come?"

"I was curious," admitted Mabel.

Gwen laughed. "That's so bizarre, even Robbie might think it's funny." Smiling, Gwen didn't look so tired. A cup of tea would bring color. A bowl of rice, white cabbage, an egg, or a little meat. She was thin but strong. Her hands were now like Mabel's, resting like birds in her skirted lap. She looked at the kitchen clock. "Dewey will be here in five. You better go."

"Do you see your husband?" asked Mabel.

"Every other month. Robbie wants me to come more often, but I've got Dewey. I don't like a lot of his friends. I don't have any place to leave him." She gripped her arms at the elbows. "He's eleven. His friends call him Do-It. I hate that."

Mabel stood up to leave. She looked around the kitchen. It was very clean. There was a school picture—a boy, stuck to the refrigerator with an apple-shaped magnet. She made out a sketch of dark eyes, like his mother's, but she couldn't see the expression.

"May I look?" she asked and walked closer to peer. "My eyes," she explained. "Sometimes I have to ask strangers to read me bus numbers and road signs. He looks like a good boy."

"Dewey loves Chinese food," offered Gwen, "but we never know where to go. Do you have any children?"

"A son," said Mabel, "and my daughter Carolee."

"I'm sorry about your husband," said Gwen. Mabel felt bad. It hadn't occurred to her to say the same.

It had been Wendell's idea to clear out his father's books. C.K. had hundreds. Dictionaries, repair manuals, poetry, history, politics. Legal texts long outdated, law school casebooks too old to be of use to anyone. Most he had bought used, in the dusty stalls of downtown book dealers. He never read a single volume, though he always stamped his name in each book. Front cover, back cover, random pages in between. He'd had a special stamp made up, self-inking, he said proudly, showing Mabel how it worked. C.K. Fong, Attorney-at-Law, with their home address beneath.

Mabel's job was to box up the books, first crossing out the stamps with a thick black marker. Wendell took the boxes around to sell. A lot of the books the dealers didn't want back. Wendell gave those away. The library took some and a shelter or two. A letter arrived. "An answer," Mabel thought, as though she had written first and expected a reply.

"Dear C.K. Fong: I am an inmate at the Chino state correctional facility. I got your name from a law book that came to our library. It was a mistake for me to get convicted for robbery and aggravated assault. My lawyer did a lousy job on my case. He did not use a witness who was with me the night this all happened. I am in here for another two years if I don't get help from a better lawyer. If you can help me, will you please contact my wife. Her name is Gwen Rattle, she lives in San Francisco too. Thank you. Yours sincerely."

It took Mabel an hour to read it. The handwriting was bad, and her magnifying glass kept fogging. Rob Rattle, or was it Roy? Roy sounded more criminal. The stamp on the front, she read that clearly enough. INMATE MAIL, in red across the bottom. The envelope was slit and taped back up. One corner had a hole as big as her thumb. Mabel took out her own tape and made a careful repair.

"Toss it," he would have said, if she had shown Wendell the letter. He came once a week to pat her sloping shoulder and go through her mail. She made him a tea tray and sliced up fresh fruit; to the side of the plate she laid the statements and bills. "Make it last, Mom," he frequently cautioned. "You're going to live a long, long time." A prediction from Wendell always sounded like a threat.

She lived on the second floor. Wendell rang twice as she was getting to the door.

"I brought you these from the country." He handed her a big brown sack. When he let go, it almost slipped from her grasp.

"Tomatoes," he said with satisfaction.

"I'll make you tomato pepper beef." She hefted the bag for show. She knew it was a test—a heavy sack, the stairs to climb. He still had a key; he could have let himself in or at least waited till they got to the kitchen.

"I've got plans. I just wanted to check in." He looked at his watch, then glanced at himself in the hallway mirror. He had his father's supple skin and his handsome features too—high forehead, narrow jaw, a crest of film-star cheekbones. When they got married—Mabel at thirty-two and C.K. twenty months younger—the photographer kept snapping pictures of C.K., almost forgetting the whey-faced bride. "What a catch," he'd said to Mabel with a wink, but C.K. overheard and made rubbery faces at the camera after that. *He* never expected gratitude, though everyone else remarked for years afterward on her astonishing good luck.

Wendell's full name was Oliver Wendell Fong; his friends called him Dell. Mabel disliked the nickname—so blunt, so American, like something out of a comic book or the ugly novels she saw women reading on the bus—but she couldn't get him to change it back.

"No offense," he declared when he went away to college. "I'm shedding the name you guys gave me. It reeks of parental aspiration." Now and then she paid him back by using his Chinese name in public. She had her little tests too.

At the end of the hall was Mabel's tiny kitchen. She rattled pots and pans, making room for Wendell's sack.

"Why did you bring me so many?" She laid the tomatoes on the counter, a dozen bright red fruits stemmed in prickly green. Vine, she smelled, and acid warmth.

"I thought you might like them in salads."

They tantalized; if Wendell weren't watching, she would have picked one up and bitten into it like an apple. She missed the pleasures of opening up and clamping down. Maybe this softer, more forgiving flesh would give way to even her rubbled teeth. They were down to the nubs now, shored up from one end of her jaw to the other with beautiful gold bridgework. The most gold she ever owned was all in her mouth. In China, she remembered, her uncle had paid her family's wartime rent in ingots of gold. Her father had raged and tried to refuse it, but her mother took it up and walked rapidly through the streets. Mabel pushed half the tomatoes into the bag and thrust it back at Wendell.

"Too many," she said.

"That's one of the great things about the Towers. You won't have to deal with cooking for just one." He wanted her to leave the flat—after thirty-nine years!—and move to a building across the Bay. "Senior living," they called it, with a common dining room and a smiling lady at the front desk.

"No stairs either," he added. As if she hadn't just climbed them, all fourteen, with a heavy package in one hand and her foolish son watching every step!

"The stairs! Weren't you paying attention?"

Wendell shrugged. "I'm just saying it's convenient. For everyone. That's all."

Carolee worked a few blocks from the Towers. She and Wendell had visited the place twice. They had picked out a fifth-floor unit, vacant at the end of the month. Wendell wanted to pay her first and last month's rent, but Carolee—not pretty, but so much smarter than the boy!—told him to be quiet. We're not going to push her, Mabel heard her whisper when she left the room for more tea.

"A lot of Chinese in the building, Mom," Carolee had called to the kitchen. "They serve noodles Sunday dinner!"

Wendell sat down and spread the mail on the kitchen table. "Did you get the mutual fund statement yet?"

"This is everything." The secrecy pleased her. There wasn't much Wendell didn't know these days about her savings, her taxes, her health. He had tried twice to talk to her about hormone therapy, "so you won't get shorter than you already are." She had pretended not to hear. And now she had the letter, hidden in C.K.'s desk.

"You can go," she said abruptly. Wendell looked up in surprise. "There's nothing important today."

"I can stay a little longer," he said.

"Go now, stay longer next time." She quickly collected the tomatoes and his coat. When she heard the front door click at the bottom of the stairs, she hurried back to C.K.'s desk. Her knees cracked as she knelt to the floor, and she scraped her wrist, groping toward the back of the bottommost drawer. Foolish old woman!

She could have left it right on top. In the six years since C.K. had passed, Wendell had never sat in the chair or fingered his father's things. "Nothing I need," he told his mother, when she offered to let him go through it. Carolee had chosen her father's eyeglasses and one stone chop. They cried together when she picked up the glasses, then tried them on, doing imitations of his bad Jack Benny—*RAH-chester*—slapping their palms to laughing faces.

"To C.K. Fong, Attorney-at-Law." Mabel touched the envelope and smiled. C.K. had used the title for forty-five years, though he made his living working for other people, renting out apartments to respectable Chinese. "Who wants a foreign lawyer?" he said when she cautiously asked him on their fifth date why he didn't have an office. He warned her about money, how slowly it would come. Risk and adventure had scared him more than most. Mabel studied the name at the bottom of the letter. The next day, she called Gwen Rattle.

Mabel let a week pass after her first visit. She shopped in the markets and packed a few more books. Seven days seemed a courteous time to wait. When she telephoned again, Gwen called her Mabel.

"Five Happiness," Mabel advised. She wanted Gwen to know where to take Dewey for a good Chinese meal. In Chinatown, across from the Wells Fargo Bank. She told her where to park, what to order. Later, Gwen called back to say how much they liked it. Dewey loved the tomato pepper beef!

Could I make him some, Mabel asked, and bring it over? Why not? Mabel was pleased to do that for Dewey. Gwen said he was a good student. She imagined he would send her a thank-you note: "I loved the Chinese food. Will you teach my mom how to make it?"

Gwen worked in an office—a systems repair dispatch service, she called it—starting at six and home by three to meet Dewey. Her office was near Chinatown. At lunchtime, Mabel took her around, pointing out the best markets and teaching her how to argue with the grocers. She went to Gwen's in the afternoons to show her how to cook what they had purchased. Gwen surprised her again; she was good at the stove. She had anise stars in her cupboard, so they didn't need to buy them for the red-cooked beef. Two weeks passed, then two more. Wendell was annoyed that Mabel wasn't packing. Carolee noticed Mabel's pep.

"I wish I had your energy, Mom," Carolee commented.

"But you haven't made much progress on the books," said Wendell.

"It takes so long to hunt for all the stamps. Maybe I should skip that part and just pack them up."

"No, don't skip that. You can't be too careful about giving out your address. Even though you'll be moving."

Carolee frowned at her brother.

"I'll be careful," promised Mabel, although there was no need to worry. Gwen Rattle had turned out to be fun. Mabel was even a little disappointed. Modern life, modern safety, was mostly about dumb luck. She wanted to push against something more than luck. She wanted to test whatever keenness was left in her against something that might push back.

Dewey had pushed her, a little. At first, when Mabel and Gwen cooked, he stayed away from the kitchen. He was tall and underfed, with Gwen's thick hair and a full mouth he shut tight around Mabel. Mabel was sorry for Gwen, that her son wasn't more polite.

"My father's in the joint," he said to her rudely one afternoon, when he got home from school and found Mabel cooking. He made a sound with his curvy lips. "Mom drives down there to tell him lies about me."

"Dewey—" started Gwen, but Mabel interrupted.

"My father was kidnapped by bandits," she said nonchalantly. She saw his eyes flick. To him, she was an old woman, as wrinkled as the dried red fruit displayed in the Chinatown markets. But she had stories. That gave her the edge.

"He was kidnapped one night, when I was a very young girl, and my family was living in the south. Bandits took him into the mountains. They sent a message, demanding money. My mother worked for three years getting together the ransom. She borrowed against our land and sold everything else. Finally, she had the money. She sent it to the bandits, but my father was already on his way home. He had escaped a month earlier, one night when the bandits got drunk."

"What happened to the money?"

"I suppose the bandits got it, or somebody else stole it. My father was very angry at what my mother had done. Look at this," she said to Gwen, holding up a tomato. "My son brings me these from the country." Gwen took it and held it to her nose.

"Fabulous," she said.

"But he makes such a big deal about it, sometimes I want to throw one at his head." They laughed. Dewey stayed with them to tip green beans while they cooked. They had a party: six dishes, three people. Wendell had been right. It was always better to cook for more than one.

On Wednesday, eight weeks after they'd become friends, Gwen called up Mabel.

"I have a big favor to ask. I promised Robbie I'd get down to see him this weekend. Dewey was supposed to stay at a friend's, but now the friend's been grounded and I don't want him there. Can he stay with you, Mabel?" Mabel heard her swallow.

"What does Dewey say?" Wendell was due to come by this weekend, to read the mail and fix a leaky faucet.

"I told him you'd make all his favorite dishes. I'm sorry to even ask."

"Please," said Mabel. "Let Dewey stay here."

"Come for dinner Sunday night," she told Wendell when he called. He was going to the country on Saturday, he said, and would come over on Sunday with his tools. "You can meet my weekend guest."

"Where will you put a guest?" The house was all boxes now; Carolee had begun to spend her spare time packing up the books, old clothes, good dishes. To give you more room, Mom, she'd explained.

"He'll sleep in your old room. I've cleared a little space by the bed."

"He?"

"A friend's grandson," lied Mabel. "The parents are away, and she's having minor surgery tomorrow." It sounded preposterous. It would be interesting, after all, if Wendell found out. Something might happen. Something might push back.

——— ═══════

When they arrived on Saturday, Dewey followed his mother up the stairs, looking blankly ahead, saying nothing. Gwen was all chatter. She would pick him up tomorrow night and bring him a hug from his father. Was there anything else he needed? She'd be back soon, she promised. Gwen's cheeks were so pink, Mabel almost felt them with the back of her hand.

"Be good, will you please, for Mabel."

"We have a lot of cooking to do," said Mabel. "We don't want you rushing back." Dewey nodded, mumbling something at his feet. He gave his mother a little wave and disappeared into the living room while Mabel saw Gwen to the stairs.

"Who's that?" Dewey asked when Mabel joined him. He was looking at a picture on the shelf.

"My father." She nodded, and Dewey lifted down the photograph so they could look at it together. Her father looked foreign even to Mabel, in a queue and mortified smile.

"Is this the guy who got kidnapped?"

"Yes, but that didn't happen until later. After I was born."

"So is he still around?"

"My father? He'd be ancient!"

"How old are you?" asked Dewey.

"Old," said Mabel firmly.

"I guess," said Dewey.

"But not ancient."

"What's it like?" asked Dewey.

"*RAH-chester*," replied Mabel, slapping her hand to her cheek. "*Tell the kid I'm only thirty-nine.*"

Dewey laughed. "Whatever you say, Mrs. Fong."

"Hi kids," said Wendell. He was smiling too. She hadn't heard him slip up the stairs.

"What are you doing here today?" she demanded.

"I thought you might need help with dinner. I brought you more tomatoes." He held up another sack, bulging.

"Bring them into the kitchen. This is Dewey," she added over her shoulder, steaming toward the kitchen, her indignation telegraphed in the slap of her slippers.

"Hi, Dewey. Who's Dewey again?"

Dewey twitched his curvy lips. He snapped his fingers in front of Wendell's face, as if to say "hel-loooo."

"Dewey's a friend."

Wendell smiled warily.

"How do you know my mom, Dewey?"

"She and my dad are pen pals." Dewey was patient when he said this, studying the wall.

"Pen pals?"

"I got a letter from his father," explained Mabel.

"I didn't see that in the mail."

"No, you didn't."

"Who's your father, Dewey?"

"Inmate number 629." It wasn't the right number, but Mabel didn't correct him.

"Excuse me?"

"*Jail mail*, Wendell," said Mabel. "That's what I got from Dewey's father. Actually, it was addressed to Dad."

Wendell stood. He walked around the kitchen once.

"That's a new one, Mom." He decided to laugh. He took another turn around the kitchen, small as it was.

"I'm pleased to meet you, Dewey." He held out his hand, but Dewey didn't take it, so Wendell reached into the brown bag and took out a tomato.

"Do you like tomatoes, Dewey?" He took a deep sniff, then lifted it to Dewey's nose. "Have you ever smelled anything like that? They're grown in the country, at a little truck farm I know. My mother is a good cook. She loves these." He was smiling at the boy, still holding out the tomato.

"My mother is a very good cook." He paused. "Would you like to watch the game while she's cooking?"

Dewey took the tomato from Wendell's hand. He was standing stiffly, the way his mother had stood in the doorway the first time Mabel showed up, the way Mabel sometimes found herself standing next to Wendell when he read through her mail. His lips had flattened to a thin pink line. Dewey looked over at Mabel, lifting the tomato in his hand. She nodded. He threw the tomato as hard as he could; it burst against the wall, filling her kitchen with the wonderful scent of the bountiful garden.

"Jesus, Dewey!" yelled Wendell, but he didn't grab the boy, because his mother was yelling too, in Chinese, at Wendell, telling him to leave Dewey alone. Red seeded liquid trickled down the kitchen wall, dripping behind her stove. It was going to be hard to reach it when she went to clean it up.

"Who is this delinquent?" shouted Wendell. "He's dangerous!" He took his mother's shoulder in his widespread hand. She pushed at him, and he backed into the hallway, onto the first step.

"Go now," she told him.

"What did I do?"

"You want so much from me!" cried Mabel.

"Only a little thanks. A little gratitude." He reached again for his mother. One arm was up, and his long, elegant feet crowded the narrow step. She had never, in all the years of holding him high to the light or turning him around to face his laughing father, handled her son with anything but love, but now she pushed him, as hard as she could, and stood silent while he tumbled down the stairs. Dewey was waiting, keeping quiet in the kitchen. She remembered how her mother had cried when her father had come home at last. He found them in their oldest clothes, cooking out of one pot in a house emptied of its treasures. Stupid woman! he shouted, his fleshless arm upraised. He dragged her out in the open to beat her, so all the neighbors would see. You've left me a poor, poor man! He cursed her with a swollen tongue, hawking dark spittle between the blows. Her mother did not fight back, though she could have thrown him off with one glorious push. What did I do so wrong? she wailed. I thought you would be grateful!

Mabel descended the stairs with care, as slowly as she did when no one was watching. Wendell was weeping, the poor, stupid boy. She lowered herself beside him onto the bottom step. Her slippered feet were next to his shoulders, her hands in her lap could reach, if she wanted, to pat the tears from his handsome face. She would do that for him if he didn't ask her why. Wendell lifted his head to speak. She gave him a look, as tender as one could give. A test, of sorts, yet then again, it wasn't. Either way she would comfort him.

Mrs. Zhao
and
Mrs. Wu

Mrs. Zhao must return to China. Cynthia does not want to think about it. She will have to start looking all over again for someone to replace her, and when is she going to find the time to do that? She will have to run an ad, or at least post a notice at the vegetable market, because she's certainly not going to get lucky again, not like she did with Mrs. Zhao. A little slip of paper pushed into their mailbox—"Chinese lady, 50, looking for work," with Mrs. Zhao's name and telephone number. She will have to post a notice; she'll need her friend Sharon's help to write it out. And then the women will call, and she will have to find a way to screen them over the phone, apologizing all the while for her atrocious accent. The phone is much harder, because she can't use her hands. She needs her hands to get her point across.

Mrs. Zhao does not want to leave. She has a good job, a California driver's license. But she must go back to see her uncle. He is dying of cancer, or if not cancer, a tumor or maybe ulcers. Cynthia is not too sure. The uncle has two nephews, both here, and Mrs. Zhao. Naturally she is the one for it. She can cook for him, bathe him, hold the rice bowl up to his mouth. Her husband does not mind. She will be back in a month, maybe two months, and in the meantime, their daughter will take care of him.

Cynthia could call an agency. Most of her friends do that. Cynthia has seen the results. Young American women, resting between semesters. Who need the money. Who are willing, if the money is right and the hours aren't too long and the mother doesn't want much in the way of cooking or cleaning or laundry, to come into your home on a daily basis for the care and feeding of children and pets. Cynthia would rather have Mrs. Zhao.

She has not yet told the children. They like Mrs. Zhao well enough, but maybe they will not be too upset? Mrs. Zhao is too Chinese, they tell her. Cynthia reminds her children that they are Chinese too. It does not send them to the mirror. They know what they look like, but they do not feel Chinese.

Mrs. Zhao has been good to Cynthia's children. She spends most of her time bending down to them, checking eyes, ears, nose, throat. Is there enough light for reading? Put on this hat when we go to the park. Peter is six; she still wipes his nose. Wear a scarf too, if it's windy. Sometimes she does the shopping right before she meets them at the bus stop, and when they get off, she's waiting for them with treats. They dig for the boxes from her pink plastic bags. Panda-head cookies with chocolate cream. Sugar rolls they brandish like cigarettes, tapping out the crumbs for ashes. Cynthia once read the box labels and groaned. Everything with palm oil, the worst kind. She asked Mrs. Zhao to buy minibagels instead, or the low-fat granola bars, this kind, with the red printing on the box. Mrs. Zhao nodded hard. The next week, panda heads again.

Cynthia's husband, Martin, will certainly miss Mrs. Zhao. He loves her *ma po tofu*. She also does a beautiful job with his blue denim shirt. She would iron all the white ones too, but he takes those to the laundry down the block because Mrs. Wong, who owns the laundry, would worry about him if he didn't show up on Mondays. He never sends Mrs. Zhao to the laundry. He doesn't want to upset Mrs. Wong.

Cynthia's friend, Sharon, thinks Cynthia has struck gold in Mrs. Zhao. But Sharon speaks fluently, and her kids do too, since they spend every summer with relatives in Taipei. Cynthia's relatives are all here. Sharon's mother takes care of Sharon's children. I'd give anything to have a Mrs. Zhao, says Sharon, but my mother would never forgive me.

Cynthia's mother and Cynthia's mother-in-law have mixed feelings about Mrs. Zhao. She is a good cook, that is true. She is patient with their grandchildren. But they each have had their run-ins with Mrs. Zhao. On her last visit, Cynthia's mother asked Mrs. Zhao to hold back just a little on the dried red peppers, or the pork sauce noodles would be *tai la* for the children. Mrs. Zhao did not appreciate the suggestion. And when Cynthia's mother-in-law let the children play the board game Junior Labyrinth every night at the dinner table, the week Cynthia and Martin went to the Caribbean, Mrs. Zhao made a formal protest to Cynthia the very night they came home. She had said nothing to Mrs. Chang, she wanted to assure Cynthia of that. It was not her place to speak to Mr. Martin's mother. But did Cynthia know what was going on in there, at the table? The children were playing games while they ate their supper. It was bad for their *qi*, their energy. Their digestive juices would not flow properly. Cynthia kissed her children hello and put away their game. Mrs. Zhao bore a stack of dirty plates to the kitchen like a silver cup.

Cynthia will have to look for someone new, and soon. Mrs. Zhao is leaving in two weeks.

Mrs. Zhao has good news—she has found a replacement! Her daughter knows a lady, very fine lady, who can take the job. Her name is Mrs. Wu. Mrs. Zhao's daughter is a friend of Mrs. Wu's niece. She is a good lady. She can cook, clean house, watch the children. Mrs. Zhao will show her how to make *ma po tofu* the way Mr. Martin likes it. She will tell her to hold back a little on the dried red peppers in the pork sauce noodles. It is all arranged. Mrs. Wu can start the day after Mrs. Zhao leaves.

Cynthia is relieved; she likes Mrs. Wu. She likes Mrs. Wu even better than Mrs. Zhao. For one thing, her English is a little better. She has been here longer, and she's from Hong Kong, not China, so appliances aren't so daunting. She has already mastered the bread machine and the can opener. Mrs. Zhao never did learn the can opener; and the bread machine, Cynthia didn't even buy until after Mrs. Zhao was gone. Cynthia had been wanting to get one forever so that her children, coming home from school, would smell fresh-baked bread in the house. She had been right to buy it. The children devour a loaf every afternoon. At six thirty, when Cynthia and Martin walk in, the smell of the bread still lingers. Mrs. Zhao would not have approved. She had little use for bread.

Mrs. Wu makes great *ma po tofu*. She goes to the laundry because she knows Mrs. Wong. They are in the same social club, and their children went to the same schools. On Mondays, Martin can sleep in an extra fifteen minutes or leave early and have time for the gym at lunch. Mrs. Wu even does Cynthia's hand wash, five pairs of stockings a week. She soaks them in the laundry room sink, then rinses them gently and hangs them up to dry. Once, Mrs. Zhao put them in the dryer. Four pairs at $8.50 apiece, and the fifth, the DKNY opaques, at $14.50. Cynthia can trust Mrs. Wu to do better.

The children like Mrs. Wu just fine. She brings them treats less often, but she doesn't zip up their jackets the minute they step off the bus. She still wipes Peter's nose though. They have stopped asking about Mrs. Zhao, about when she is coming back from China.

Cynthia feels she must find out, before she makes a more permanent arrangement with Mrs. Wu. The two months have gone by, and she has had no word from Mrs. Zhao. She calls Mrs. Zhao's daughter. Not to worry, says her daughter. Mother is not coming back anytime soon. Uncle is hanging on, and mother is needed. She does not expect to come home for at least a year. She must have some minor surgery herself, some woman problems, and she would rather do it in China, where the doctors are paid for. Do not wait for Mother. She told me so last week.

Cynthia speaks to Mrs. Wu, offers her full-time, long-term employment, with benefits. Mrs. Wu happily accepts. Cynthia sits down with her to go over the contract, only she does not call it a contract because she does not want to appear heavy-handed. It is a "working agreement." It sets out everything about the job so there will be no misunderstandings down the road. Mrs. Wu cannot disagree. She will be paid quite well for eleven hours a day, five days a week. She will get a health insurance allowance and eight paid holidays. Most families give only seven, but Cynthia and Martin give Martin Luther King Jr. Day too, because they believe it is only right. She will get two weeks of paid vacation a year, as long as Mrs. Wu takes her vacation at the same time as Cynthia, Martin, and the children take theirs. Mrs. Wu signs where indicated.

Mrs. Wu is sorry, very, very sorry, but she will have to leave. Mrs. Zhao has returned from China this week and wants her old job back. She called Mrs. Wu on the phone last night. She says she will need a few days to rest and then she will come. She asks Mrs. Wu to tell the family: Mrs. Zhao is back from China.

Cynthia is dismayed. There is no reason for Mrs. Wu to go. Cynthia had called Mrs. Zhao's daughter; the daughter told Cynthia not to wait. Mrs. Zhao has been gone nine months. She cannot have thought Cynthia would hold her job open for nine months. Cynthia does not want Mrs. Wu to go.

Mrs. Wu is sorry, but she will have to leave. Mrs. Zhao is home and wants her old job back.

Cynthia calls Mrs. Zhao on the telephone. It is not fair to Mrs. Wu. Mrs. Zhao did not say when she would be coming back. Her daughter told Cynthia to go ahead and hire Mrs. Wu. Mrs. Wu has been working hard for nine months. Cynthia cannot ask Mrs. Wu to go.

Ah, ah, ah. Mrs. Zhao listens but she does not give anything away. I am back now, is all she says to Cynthia. China was very cold.

Martin tells Cynthia to let it go. Give Mrs. Zhao her job back and send Mrs. Wu a nice severance check. Maybe Cynthia can find her another family, post it on e-mail at the office. Don't put her in a bad position. Let her go, but give her some money too.

Cynthia disagrees. Don't I have any say in this, she tells her husband. Mrs. Zhao cannot arrange this without talking to me first. What makes Cynthia so mad is that, on the phone, Mrs. Zhao would not admit that she had called Mrs. Wu before she talked to Cynthia. Mrs. Zhao must have known that Mrs. Wu had told Cynthia that Mrs. Zhao told Mrs. Wu to go. Otherwise, how would Cynthia have known to call Mrs. Zhao?

Don't put Mrs. Wu in a bad position, says Martin. She doesn't want to cause problems between her niece and Mrs. Zhao's daughter.

No, says Cynthia. I will explain to Mrs. Wu that she does not have to go.

Mrs. Zhao has her old job back. The panda-head cookies are back and the red pepper in the pork sauce. Everything is as it was. Cynthia calls her friend Sharon, relates the whole saga. Sharon laughs. I can't tell you how Chinese that story is, she says.

THE IOWA SHORT FICTION AWARD AND JOHN SIMMONS SHORT
FICTION AWARD WINNERS, 1970–2009

Donald Anderson
Fire Road
Dianne Benedict
Shiny Objects
David Borofka
Hints of His Mortality
Robert Boswell
Dancing in the Movies
Mark Brazaitis
*The River of Lost Voices:
Stories from Guatemala*
Jack Cady
*The Burning and Other
Stories*
Pat Carr
The Women in the Mirror
Kathryn Chetkovich
Friendly Fire
Cyrus Colter
The Beach Umbrella
Jennine Capó Crucet
How to Leave Hialeah
Jennifer S. Davis
Her Kind of Want
Janet Desaulniers
What You've Been Missing
Sharon Dilworth
The Long White
Susan M. Dodd
Old Wives' Tales
Merrill Feitell
*Here Beneath
Low-Flying Planes*
James Fetler
Impossible Appetites
Starkey Flythe, Jr.
Lent: The Slow Fast
Sohrab Homi Fracis
*Ticket to Minto: Stories of
India and America*

H. E. Francis
The Itinerary of Beggars
Abby Frucht
Fruit of the Month
Tereze Glück
*May You Live in Interesting
Times*
Ivy Goodman
Heart Failure
Ann Harleman
Happiness
Elizabeth Harris
The Ant Generator
Ryan Harty
*Bring Me Your Saddest
Arizona*
Mary Hedin
Fly Away Home
Beth Helms
American Wives
Jim Henry
*Thank You for Being
Concerned and Sensitive*
Lisa Lenzo
Within the Lighted City
Kathryn Ma
*All That Work and
Still No Boys*
Renée Manfredi
Where Love Leaves Us
Susan Onthank Mates
The Good Doctor
John McNally
Troublemakers
Molly McNett
One Dog Happy
Kevin Moffett
Permanent Visitors
Lee B. Montgomery
Whose World Is This?